PILPAY'S FABLES

PILPAY'S FABLES

by

SIR RICHARD BURTON

Orchid Press
Bangkok 2003

Sir Richard Burton
Pilpay's Fables

Edited by Thomas E. Cox
With illustrations by Sushiela Goodwin

Orchid Press,
P.O. Box 19,
Yuttitham Post Office,
Bangkok 10907, Thailand

This book is printed on acid-free long life paper
which meets the specifications of ISO 9706 / 1994

ISBN 974-524-028-1

CONTENTS

EDITOR'S FOREWORD

Discovery

In 1995, while working in Nepal, I was reading Fawn Brodie's biography of Sir Richard Burton (for the second time). In a footnote Brodie casually mentioned that (as of 1967 when her biography came out) Burton's translation of *Pilpay's Fables* was still unpublished and being kept in the Royal Anthropological Institute in London. By that time I had become an absolute Burton fanatic and was immediately buying and studying anything about, or by, Burton as soon as it became available. (I was doing this because of my personal idolatry of Burton himself and also because I was applying his research and writing techniques to my own anthropological work in Nepal.) I had been keeping very careful track of the Burton writings that had been published, reprinted, et cetera. These, of course, included all of Burton's travel books, ethnographic accounts and translations (except for Pilpay's Fables). I also knew there was some Burton material (his letters, for example) that were still unpublished. When I read that footnote for the second time it was like being struck by lightning. I knew, almost intuitively, that a great opportunity to publish Burton's first translation, for the first time, had, possibly, just dropped in my lap.

A day or two later I called the Royal Anthropological Institute and inquired about *Pilpay's Fables*. They informed me that their entire collection of Burton manuscripts had keen sold to the Huntington Library (in San Marino, California) and that the translation was still unpublished. I then called the Huntington Library and received confirmation that they had *Pilpay's Fables*; both the original handwritten manuscript and a typescript. I inquired right away if it would be possible for me to publish it. They said for this to happen I would have to have a publisher lined up and submit a proposal and modest publication fee. Within a matter of weeks the necessary arrangements had been made and a copy of the translation was in my possession.

After I decided to publish *Pilpay's Fables* my research into Burton's life and work expanded, and also became more focused, the goal being, of course, to write an introduction to the translation, one that discussed Burton's incredible contributions to anthropology and the special qualities that made his translations so important. I knew that Burton's biographers had not really done this, in part, because they were not anthropologists themselves. I only attained an understanding of the significance of Burton's ethnography after comparing him to other anthropologists and actually applying his research techniques when I was researching Nepal's commercial sex industry as a consultant for Family Health International.

No American academic anthropologist

has written a book, or even an in-depth article about Burton's work in anthropology. This neglect has been due to the counterproductive politics and attitudes that plague American academic anthropology. Unofficially, in casual conversation, American anthropology professors freely acknowledge that Burton was a great pioneering anthropologist. Officially, however, Burton is ignored. His work is never cited. His books are never assigned readings for students. Why? Currently, most academic anthropologists in the USA produce extremely theoretical, abstract articles and books that are more anthropological philosophy than real ethnography. They don't write the richly detailed, empirical, ethnographically authoritative accounts that Burton did because, quite simply, most of them can't. They just do not have the necessary linguistic or ethnographic fieldwork skills. This means that if they officially recognize and promote Burton's work they will, implicitly, be showing the world just how inadequate and misguided their own work is. This, of course, is the last thing they want to do. They want to preserve the mystique, the myth, that real, professional level anthropology can only be done by Ph.D. holding academics.

Another reason Burton is officially ignored by academics is that his work is not politically correct. It is true that Burton could, at times, be very racist. But that does not detract from the value of his work. However, in this politically correct age that

is just not good enough for some people.

All of Burton's brilliance is on full display in his translation of *Pilpay's Fables*. Knowing the history of this translation enables us to understand just how special and significant it is.

The Translation

Burton was only 26 years old when he translated *Pilpay's Fables* in Bombay (see Brodie 1984; 68) and Ootacamund (a town on India's west coast) in 1847 (see Burton 1992; 311). This handwritten translation remained in Burton's possession until his death in 1890. (Why Burton never published it is a mystery.) After that it was kept for many years by the Royal Anthropological Institute in London. It is amazing that the translation has been preserved. It survived an 1861 warehouse fire (that destroyed many of Burton's other manuscripts), Isabel Burton's deliberate burning of Burton's journals and other writings, bombings during World War II and even a flood in a library basement (see Brodie 1984; 68).

Burton's translation is a stunning scholarly achievement, one that surpasses all other renderings (see, for example, Eastwick 1984; Irving 1980 and Keith-Falconer 1970) of Pilpay's Fables. The superiority of Burton's translation is due, primarily, to his linguistic and ethnographic expertise.

By the time Burton began translating *Pilpay's Fables* he had learned Hindi,

Persian and Sanskrit (see Brodie 1984). Burton's mastery of these languages made it possible for him to study and compare different versions of *Pilpay's Fables*. It also enabled him to produce an extremely accurate translation that preserves the meaning, style, tone and charm of the original stories.

Burton also had a deep understanding of the different cultural contexts in which the fables were composed, translated and altered. This gave Burton an insight that no other western scholar had. Burton included these insights in fascinating footnotes, 176 in all, that appear throughout his translation. (A small number of these refer on to an appendix— apparently now lost or destroyed—while these are not of practical use to the present reader, they have still been retained in this publication, in an attempt to remain as true as possible to Burton's original work.)

Preparing *Pilpay's Fables* for publication presented some special challenges, both scholarly and technical. The most formidable task was educating myself about the fables and Burton's life and work. This required extensive reading, analysis and discussions with linguists, anthropologists and writers. On the technical side there was the challenge of printing the Sanskrit terms that Burton wrote, in Devanagri script, alongside their English translations. This hurdle was overcome by using special computer programs that print both Devanagri and Roman script.

Burton's translation has been presented here exactly as it appears in the original handwritten manuscript (see Burton #104x. 1847). The translation, in parts, is a little "rough". For example, Burton labelled the first fable (Mitra Labha) as chapter one. After that the text just flows from one story to the next, with no additional chapter headings. What must be emphasized here is that Burton's chapter one means all the fables in their entirety. There simply is no chapter two, three, etc. in Burton's translation. Another "irregularity" is Burton's spelling, which is a little erratic, not only in *Pilpay's Fables*, but in all of his books as well. This, however, does not detract from the clarity and readability of any of Burton's translations or ethnographies.

For enhanced readibility, words underlined by Burton and verse quotes have been changed to italics. Also, each chapter starts on a new page and with a bold heading, whereas in Burton's original the text flowed with no breaks for new "chapters".

The publication of *Pilpay's Fables* is the culmination of several years of hard work. All of this, however, has been a labor of love. It is my sincere wish that *Pilpay's Fables* will be enjoyed by readers everywhere and inspire people to learn the valuable lessons Burton has to teach us about how to understand, and become more sensitive to, other cultures.

Thomas E. Cox
Nagoya, Japan, 2003

EDITOR'S INTRODUCTION

The stories in *Pilpay's Fables* are very old. Exactly how old nobody can say with certainty. However, *Pilpay's Fables* come from another collection of Indian stories known as the Hitopadesa. The stories in the Hitopadesa were apparently written down sometime between CE 800 and CE 1373 by a scholar named Narayani (Sternbach 1960; 2). However, at least seventy-five per cent of the stories in the Hitopadesa are not original. They were taken from an even older Indian text known as the Panchatantra (see Sternbach 1960; 1).

While it is not known exactly how old the Panchatantra is, some scholars believe that it may have been written around 200 BCE (see Ryder 1925; 3-4 and Upadhyay 1971; 6). But many stories in the Panchatantra were probably passed down, by oral tradition, long before they were written (see Upadhyay 1971).

In the introduction to Burton's translation of *Pilpay's Fables* the author states that Nasir Un Din (a ruler of the Indian state of Bihar) had the fables translated into Persian, and that this text was then translated into Hindi (in CE 1802) by a man named Bahadur Ali-I-Husain, on the order of one John Gilchrist Esq. (Burton #104a. 1847; 4).

Burton's translation of *Pilpay's Fables* begins with the story of Chandra Sain, a king who had four ignorant, ill-mannered sons. Upset by them, Chandra Sain appointed a Brahman named Bishan Sarma to educate his sons and improve both their intellect and behavior. Bishan Sarma taught the four princes by telling them *Pilpay's Fables* (Burton #104a. 1847; 1-2).

The fables are about different animals (including a crow, pigeon, vulture, mouse, deer, tortoise, jackal and cat) or people, and their relationships and various experiences. Each story is intended to teach the reader (or listener) an important lesson of life. The first story (*Mitra Labha*), for example, teaches, 'the necessity of prudence, the duties of a prince to his subjects, and the advantages of friendship in the hour of need' (Burton #104a. 1847; 6). Each fable has its own distinct characters and story line. However, all of the stories tell of an animal or person who encounters misfortune, and the lessons to be learned from this.

Since they were first written down *Pilpay's Fables* have been translated into many different languages including: Greek, Arabic, Persian, Hindi, Tibetan, Hebrew, Italian, Latin, Spanish, Turkish and German (see Keith-Falconer 1970). As previously mentioned, the Hindi text translated by Burton came from a Persian translation. And that version had probably been translated from the original Sanskrit (Burton #104a. 1847; 4).

During the process of translation the stories were changed. When *Pilpay's Fables* was translated from Sanskrit into Persian many of the originally Hindu themes, idioms' and characters were Islamicized or, more specifically, Persianized. Burton, more than any other translator, was able to identify the parts of the original Hitopadesa stories that were changed when they were translated into Persian, exactly how they were changed and, in some cases, even why they were changed. For example, in *The Tale of an Individual called Tankbir, and Naujobana the Banyan's Daughter*, there is a Banyan (a Hindu caste) man who takes his wife to meet another man. In his analysis of this story Burton (#104a. 1847; 43) writes;

The Mussalman author of this story, not wishing to introduce a brother Moslem taking his wife to another man, has made the hero of the tale and his dupe Hindus; But as usual it is full of incongruities. Banyans wear no beards, and have no day of resurrection (kiyamat), moreover they make but little distinction between mahram and na-mahram, (which I have translated 'strangers').

Burton's Linguistic Genius

Sir Richard Burton was one of nineteenth century Europe's greatest linguists. He learned at least 24 languages. These included Arabic, Armenian, Bernais, French, German, Greek, Gujarti, Hindi, Italian, Jatki, Latin, Maharati, Multani, Pashto, Persian, Portuguese, Provençal, Punjabi, Sanskrit, Sindhi, Spanish, Telugu, Turkish and, of course, English. Burton began learning European languages as a boy, when his family lived in France and Italy. As Burton grew older his passion for learning languages intensified. In 1840 and 1841, while still in England, Burton began studying Hindi and Arabic (Brodie 1984; 44-48). Later, after his arrival in India (in October of 1842),

Burton spent up to twelve hours a day studying Hindi and other Indian languages (Burton 1893; 101). In India, Burton perfected his own original technique for learning languages. This, coupled with his extraordinary natural ability, enabled Burton to learn a new language in just two months. Burton described his language learning strategy in a fragment of autobiography;

> I got a simple grammar and vocabulary, marked out the forms and words which I knew were absolutely necessary, and learnt them by heart by carrying them in my pocket and looking over them at spare moments during the day. I never worked for more than a quarter of an hour at a time, for after that the brain lost its freshness. After learning some three hundred words, easily done in a week, I stumbled through some easy book-work (one of the Gospels is the most come-atable), and underlined every word that I wished to recollect, in order to read over my pencillings at least once a day. Having finished my volume, I then carefully worked up the grammar minutiae, and I then chose some other book whose subject most interested me. The neck of the language was now broken, and progress was rapid. If I came across a new sound like the Arabic Ghayn, I trained my tongue to it by repeating it so many thousand times a day. When I read, I invariably read out loud, so that the ear might aid memory. I was delighted with the most difficult characters, Chinese and Cuneiform, because I felt that they impressed themselves more strongly upon the eye than the eternal Roman letters. Whenever I conversed with anybody in a language that I was learning, I took the trouble to repeat their words inaudibly after them, and so to learn the trick of pronunciation and emphasis. (quoted from Brodie 1967; 44).

In many of the languages he studied Burton achieved a remarkably high level of fluency. His mastery of Arabic, for example, was so complete that when Burton went (disguised as an Indian Muslim) on his celebrated pilgrimage to Mecca and Medina, none of the other Muslim pilgrims suspected that he was British (see Burton 1964).

Burton also produced highly regarded translations of literature from six different languages; Arabic (*The Arabian Nights* and *The Perfumed Garden*), Portuguese (*Camoens* and *Lacerda*), Latin (*Priapeia* and *Cattalus*), Hindi (*Pilpay's Fables* and *Vikram and the Vampire*), Italian (*Il Pentamerone*) and Sanskrit (*Ananga Ranga* and *Kama Sutra*). Burton's greatness as a translator was due not only to his linguistic ability, but also (in many cases) to his knowledge of stories in both their oral and written versions. For example, when Burton was in Arabia and Somalia, he heard the Arabian nights recited by traditional Muslim storytellers (Brodie 1984; 300). From the storytellers' speech and the reaction of the audience, Burton was better able to understand stories that he had previously read. Burton also learned to recite the Arabian Nights himself in the traditional Muslim style. Indeed, when Burton visited Bedouin (nomadic Arabs) encampments he would often recite the Arabian Nights to win the trust, respect and friendship of his Arab hosts (Burton 1962; 1-2).

Burton was also exposed to the oral and written versions of many Indian stories. In one instance Burton knew both the oral and written rendering of a Sindhi story and decided to translate the oral one because it was 'less rough and rugged'. (Burton 1992; 388).

Burton's profound understanding of stories, in both their oral and written forms, enabled him to produce translations with a deep and powerful resonance. In Burton's translations the author seems to be speaking to you from the pages. As Charles Fowkes (1992; 9) wrote in his introduction to Burton's translation of *The Perfumed Garden*; 'there is an unmistakable sense of being very close to the author when you read the book'.

Burton also had a genius for capturing the exact tone of the works he translated. Burton's profound understanding of the tone of different stories is apparent in the following passage from *The Arabian Nights*:

The general tone of the Nights is exceptionally high and pure. The devotional fervour often rises to the boiling point of fanaticism. The pathos is sweet, deep and genuine; tender, simple and true, utterly unlike much of our modern tinsel. Its life strong, splendid and multitudinous, is everywhere flavored with that unaffected pessimism and constitu-

tional melancholy (Burton 1962; 9).

While reading other translations of the *Arabian Nights* Burton saw several cases in which the particular tone of a passage had been misunderstood and consequently erroneously translated. For example, in his critique of Henry Torren's translation Burton (1962; 4-5) discussed a passage that was wrongly translated as being comical when, in fact, the tone is pathetic.

People usually learn the phonetics, grammar and vocabulary of a foreign language long before they understand the different tones or sentiments that are implicitly expressed in words or phrases. (See Brenneis 1995 for an important discussion of this subject.) Indeed, many people are never able to understand the different sentiments conveyed in a foreign language, even after years of study. Burton's uncanny ability to understand these sentiments is, in part, what enabled him to compose such exceptionally accurate translations.

Burton was not only a brilliant linguist, but a great ethnographer as well. Indeed, his achievements in these two fields were very much interrelated. Burton's linguistic ability is, to a large degree, what enabled him to success-fully conduct ethnographic research. And the ethnographic information he acquired informed and enriched all of his translations. It gave Burton a deeper understanding of idioms in a particular cultural context. Many of the footnotes in Burton's translation of *Pilpay's Fables* describe the relationship between idioms and specific beliefs and values. For example, in one footnote Burton (#104a. 1847; 10) wrote:

Amongst Asiatics, as was also the case with the Greeks and Romans, it is considered inauspicious to mention any ill-omened event too plainly. It is therefore generally merely alluded to, or sometimes hinted at by an opposite form of expression. For instance the polite way of ordering a table-cloth to be removed, is to direct the attendants to increase (the table: barhana); for fear that the inauspicious use of the word le-jana should affect the future meals. In speaking of death, sickness, failure, misfortune and many other occurrences, especially as in any way connected with the person addressed, it is only the uneducated who use the literal words.

Going Native:
Burton's Ethnographic Research

Burton's incredible linguistic ability and knowledge of other cultures enabled him to conduct ethnographic research (in India, Egypt and Arabia) while disguised as a native. Burton began doing this in 1844 while in the Sindh region of what was then Northwest India. As Burton (1852; 99) wrote;

> I began the systematic study of the Scindian people, their manners and their tongue. The first difficulty was to pass for an Oriental, and this was as necessary as it was difficult. The European official in India seldom, if ever, sees anything in its real light, so dense is the veil which the fearfulness, the duplicity, the prejudice and the superstitions of the natives hang before his eyes.

In Sindh, Burton disguised himself as Mirza Abdullah of Bushire, a wealthy merchant of Arab and Iranian parentage. Speaking fluent Sindhi and dressed in native garb and wearing long false hair and a beard, Burton was never recognized. At times he rented a shop in the main bazaar area of Karachi and would stock it with 'clammy dates, vis-cid molasses, tobacco, ginger, oil and strong smelling sweetmeats'. He would then spend days there talking about everything with everyone from priests to drug addicts. At times he would play chess with theological students. On other occasions he would drink bhang and smoke opium with the addicts. Oftentimes Burton would go from house to house displaying textiles for sale. He would talk at length with many of the Sindhis he met, heard many life histories and learned much about harems, family scandals and other aspects of Sindhi social and domestic life (see Burton 1852).

Burton's most dramatic exploit in Sindh came in 1845 when he, carefully disguised, made a thorough investigation of homosexual brothels in Karachi. Among other things Burton found out that both boys and eunuchs were available, with the former costing twice as much as the latter. The reason for this was, 'that the scrotum of the unmutilated boy could be used as a kind of bridle for directing the movements of the animal' (Burton 1962; 3854).

Perhaps Burton's most spectacularly successful disguise was that of an Indian (of Afghan parentage) Muslim doctor and dervish. With this disguise Burton went on his pilgrimage to Mecca and Medina. On several occasions he was questioned closely about his identity by Arab officials and each time he was able to meet the challenge and gain access to the most sacred sites in Islam including the Kaaba (a stone building containing the famous Black Stone), Mount Arafat and Fatimah's (Mohammed's favorite daughter) shrine. In addition, disguise enabled Burton to talk long and intimately with a wide variety of Muslims. As a result he was able to learn more about the pilgrimage, its participants and the people (including the Bedouin) around Medina and Mecca, than perhaps any other Westerner. His account of the pilgrimage remains one of the great early classics in ethnography.

Burton's disguises were always successful. As Burton expected they made it possible for him to avoid the suspicion and deception that most anthropologists must (to one extent or another) contend with. As a result Burton was able to see and learn about certain areas of native life that were often inaccessible to other Westerners. One such 'area' (as the Karachi brothel study shows) was sex. Indeed, over the course of his seven years in India, Burton

learned more about the natives' sexual behavior than any other Westerner of his time. The following passage from Burton's Terminal Essay in the Arabian Nights shows the extent of his knowledge.

> *Yet the Hindus, I repeat, hold pederasty in abhorrence and are as much scandalized by being called Gand-mara (anus-beater) or Gandu (anuser) as Englishmen would be. During the years 1843-44 ... at ... Karachi only one case of pederasty came to light and that after a tragical fashion some years afterwards. A young Brahman had connection with a soldier comrade of low caste and this had continued till, in an unhappy hour, the Pariah patient ventured to become the agent. The latter, in Arab Al-Fail = the 'doer' is not an object of contempt like Al-Maful = the 'done'; and the high-caste sepoy, stung by remorse and revenge, loaded his musket and deliberately shot his paramour.* (Burton 1962; 3669-3770).

Burton was the first British ethnographer in the Victorian era to write explicitly about sexual behavior. As W. G.

Archer (1988; 17) wrote; 'We know ... works which describe with intimate detail the place of sex in village life. In the India of 1845, no one had done this before. Burton discovered Indian sex.'

Disguise (coupled with extraordinary linguistic ability) also enabled Burton to develop his exceptional sensitivity to the emotional content of several Indian languages (and Arabic). By donning a disguise and immersing himself completely in native life for extended periods, Burton was able to bond quickly and powerfully with both Arabs and Indians. The Sindhis, for example, trusted Mirza Abdullah, they befriended Mirza Abdullah, they confided in Mirza Abdullah. Burton, for his part, by living out his fantasies, by becoming Mirza Abdullah, was able to effectively cast off the European upbringing and identity that—on a deep psychological level—were obstacles to understanding the emotional content of the natives' language and culture. Thus, there was a certain irony to Burton's disguises. By 'becoming' a native and living out his fantasies, Burton was better able to understand—and emotionally connect with—another reality; the personal, social, cultural and linguistic reality of the Arabs and Indians he lived with.

Burton's Ethnographic Writing

Burton wrote up his ethnographic research in accounts that are very empirical; filled with detailed, accurate descriptions of native life. Theoretical they are, for the most part, not. In fact Burton theorised at length only about 'African fetishism' (Brodie 1984; 332). However, it is important to realize that Burton did have great insight into other cultures and did, at times, come up with brilliant, original explanations for specific beliefs, values and patterns of behavior. His analysis of love magic in Sindh is one example.

The system of philters and amatory talismans is probably borrowed by the Moslems from the Hindoos, to whom it has long been known by the name of Washikaran. It is to the advantage of all parties to support the idea. The magician gains money by teaching his craft, the fair sex have a valid excuse when detected in a grave delinquency, and the husbands are consoled by the reflection that the chastity of their spouses could yield to none but preternatural influence (Burton 1992; 179)

Burton's writing style was as original and remarkable as his description and analyses. In the text of his books Burton describes his interactions with the natives, his various experiences, feelings and the process through which he was able to learn about another culture. Most of Burton's books also included hundreds of footnotes; so many in fact that they constitute a secondary, complementary text that runs parallel to the main one. In his footnotes Burton gives the reader a tremendous amount of factual information about the natives' culture, language and history. Thus, between the main text and the footnotes Burton was able to achieve a balance between narrative and discourse that gives the reader a comprehensive picture of a culture and Burton's experience with it.

Fortunately for us Burton was also a very productive scholar who published forty-three volumes and over one hundred articles on his research and travels. (And this does not even include his translations with their rich ethnographic data in the footnotes, introduction, etc.) Burton's books are respected not only by scholars, but also, in some cases, by the very natives they describe. For example, Burton's ethnographic account of Sindh (*Sindh and the Races That Inhabit the Valley of the Indus*) is considered, by the Sindhis themselves, to be the main reference work on the tribes and customs of Sindh. In 1986 this book was translated into Sindhi, quickly became a bestseller, and was later included in the curriculum for students (at both the graduate and undergraduate level) at the University of Sindh (Ondaatje 1996; 149-150). Burton's books on Africa are one of the most important sources of information on the African slave trade. (See Beachey 1976; Cooper 1977; Farrant 1975; Fisher and Fisher 1975 and Gemery and Hogendorn 1979 for examples of scholars of the slave trade who have drawn on Burton's work.) It is a testimony to Burton's brilliance that so many of his books are still in print, over 110 years after his death.

The Drive Behind The Disguise

An understanding of Burton's cross-cultural experiences gives us insight into not only his translations and ethnographic accounts, but Burton's personality as well. One of Burton's most important biographers, Fawn Brodie (1984; 337-8) wrote that;

The most arresting and significant aspect of Burton's life however, was his ceaseless search for an identity. We see it in his flight from self ... into languages, disguises, translation and finally into prodigious learning of a very specialized sort. But ... the desperate quest for identity as a man ... made Burton's life greater than all his books, and strangely more rewarding for us.

This conclusion is clearly wrong. Burton did not spend his life obsessively searching for one permanent identity. On the contrary, it was the ability to take on and shed several different identities that made Burton's life meaningful and exciting. Burton once wrote that learning languages made him 'independent of society' (Brodie 1984; 67). Indeed, it was Burton's linguistic ability and disguises that enabled him to make all those incredible journeys deep into the heart of different cultures and forbidden places. Burton's ability to assume different identities gave him a unique freedom. And it was this freedom that meant more to Burton than anything else.

Of the gladdest moments in human life, methinks, is the departure upon a distant journey into unknown lands. Shaking off with one mighty effort the fetters of Habit, the leaden weight of Routine, the cloak of many Cares and the Slavery of Home, man feels once more happy. The blood flows with the fast circulation of childhood ... Afresh dawns the morn of life (Burton 1872; 17-18).

Thomas E. Cox
December 2002

BIBLIOGRAPHY

Archer, W.G. 1988, 'Preface' to *The Kama Sutra of Vatsyayana* (pp. 11-42) by Arbuthnot, F.F. and Burton, Sir Richard. London: Unwin Hyman Limited.

Beachey, R.W., 1976, *A Collection Of Documents On The Slave Trade Of Eastern Africa.* London: Rex Collings.

Brenneis, Don 1995, 'Caught in the Web of Words. Performing Theory in a Fiji Indian Community.' In J. A. Russell et al. (eds), *Everyday Conceptions of Emotion* (pp. 241-250). The Netherlands: Kluwer Academic Publishers.

Brodie, Fawn, 1984, (First Published in 1967) *The Devil Drives: A Life of Sir Richard Burton.* New York: W.W. Norton and Company.

Burton, Isabel, 1893, *The Life Of Captain Sir Richard Burton.* London; Chapman and Hall.

Burton, Sir Richard, 1847, *Akhlak i Hindi: A Translation of the Hindustani Version of Pilpay's Fables.* An unpublished hand-written manuscript (Call Number #104a) in The Huntington Library, San Marino, California.

Burton, Sir Richard, 1964, (First published in 1855) *Personal Narrative Of A Pilgimage To Al-Madinah And Meccah.* New York: Dover Publications.

Burton, Sir Richard, 1992, (First published in 1851) *Goa And The Blue Mountains.* New Delhi: Asian Educational Services.

Burton, Sir Richard, 1992, (First published in 1851) *Sindh And The Races That Inhabit The Valley Of The Indus.* New Delhi: Asian Educational Services.

Burton, Sir Richard, 1852, *Falconry In The Valley Of The Indus.* London: John Van Voorst.

Burton, Sir Richard, 1872, *Zanzibar; City, Island, And Coast.* London: Tinsley Brothers.

Burton, Sir Richard, 1962, (First published in 1885) *The Book Of The Thousand Nights And A Night.* New York: The Heritage Press.

Cooper, Frederick, 1977, *Plantation Slavery On The East Coast of*

Africa. New Haven and London: Yale University Press.

Eastwick, Edward, 1984, *The Anvar-i Suhaili; Or, The Light Of Canopus; Being The Persian Version Of The Fables Of Pilpay Or The Book Of Kalilah And Damnah*. Hertford: Printed and Published by Stephen Austin.

Farrant, Leda, 1975, *Tipu Tip and the East African Slave Trade*. New York: St. Martin's Press.

Fisher, Allan G. B. and Fisher, Humphery, J., 1970, *Slaver And Muslim Society In Africa*. London: C. Hurst and Company.

Fowkes, Charles, 1992, 'Introduction' to *The Perfumed Garden* (pp. 8-9) by Burton, Sir Richard. Rochester: The Park Street Press.

Gemery, Henry A. and Hogendorn, Jan S., 1979, *The Uncommon Market: Essays In The Economic History Of The Atlantic Slave Trade*. New York: Academic Press.

Irving, Thomas, 1980, *Kalilah and Dimnah: An English Version Of Bidpai's Fables Based On Ancient Arabic, And Spanish Manuscripts*. Newark: Juan de la Cuesta.

Keith-Falconer, Ion Grant Neville, 1970, (First published in 1885) *Kalilah And Dimnah, Or The Fables Of Bidpai*. Amsterdam: Philo Press.

Ondaatje, Christopher, 1996, *Sindh Revisited: A Journey in the Footsteps of Captain Sir Richard Francis Burton 1842-1849: The India Years*. Toronto: Harper Collins Publishers.

Ryder, Arthur, 1925, *The Panchatantra*. Chicago: University of Chicago Press.

Sternbach, Ludwig, 1960, *The Hitopadesa And Its Sources*. New Haven: American Oriental Society.

Upadhyay, Asha, 1971, *Tales From India*. New York: Random House.

Akhlak-i-Hindi
or
A Translation
of the
Hindustani Version
of
Pilpay's Fables

By R. F. BURTON, Lt.
18th Regt. Bombay N.I.

With explanatory Notes, and
Appendix by the Translator

Preface
by
the Translator

The following translation is literal, "usque ad nauseam"; but it is so from necessity, not from choice. For the only purpose which an English version of the "Ethicks of India" can serve, is to assist the young Hindustani scholar in acquiring a sufficient stock of words, idioms and phrases, together with the knowledge of Oriental manners, customs and modes of thinking, necessary to enable him to attempt other and more classical works. Whenever, therefore, it has been possible, word for word has been given and any unusual deviation from the original has been explained in the Notes.

After having studied, with some success, seven Oriental dialects, the translator may be permitted to offer some advice to the beginner in Hindustani concerning his future studies; and to assure him, that a good knowledge of that language may easily be acquired in the short space of a year, by commencing with the Akhlak i Hindi then proceeding to the Tota Kahani, the Hindustani translation of Aesops Fables the Bagh o Buhar, the Gul-i-Bakawali, the Tkhwanus safa and the Ayar-i-Danish; and thence to some political author, as Mir Soz, Sanda, the Masnair or Yaajar-i-Zatalli. Secondly, that anything a fair colloquial knowledge of the Oriental Tongue, and the easily acquired capability of understanding a common note or petition, is more than likely to subject him to those unpleasant little events, which particularly affect students of Eastern literature; vix.

Evil, envy, want, the patron and the *Jail*. Thirdly and lastly, that of this ruinous study no branch is more ruinous than the classical Languages of the East;—the Persian, Sanscrit and Arabic, as the lives of Gentius & Meninski, and the death of Ockley amply prove. And at the same time we Servants of the H.E.I. Company may answer a certain remark of the learned Translator of Ibn Batuta's travels[1] by assuring him, that however vast be the means of Oriental study which the British Nation possesses, in individual capabilities of collecting Libraries, finding competent instructors, and the leisure necessary for profound study, are occasionally very limited.

The Notes, as well as the translation, here offered to the Public, will only be of use to what is termed in the Cast, a "learner of the Alif-Ba," and if they appear redundant or puerile, the error has proceeded from anxiety to avoid deficiency. The account of this most celebrated book, given in the appendix, may, it is hoped be interesting to the general reader, as well as to the student. To conclude, the attempt to put the poetical quotation into verse may be excused, as the only object was to preserve throughout the Translation, the style and spirit of the original.

Note. "A few scholars have, from time to time, appeared among the servants of the H.E.I.C.: but, when we take into account the vastness of the means which we possess together with the duty laid on us as a nation, accurately to know the condition of so many of our fellow subjects in the East, it must appear, that all which has been done, so far from being matter of exultation, must rather tend to lower in the opinion we would entertain of ourselves, and much more in that of the surrounding natives." Dedication of the travels of Ibn Batuta. P vi.

Preface
by
the Author

In the Name of God, the Compassionate, the *Merciful*.[1]

Thousands of thanksgivings to that Almighty Being, who vouchsafed unto Man superiority over the whole of His creation,—who adorned his head with the jewelled diadem of intellect, both in this world and in the next,—who mounting him upon the nimble steed of genius, and putting into his hands the reins of wisdom, intrusted to him the sword of learning, for the better management and government of the realms of the heart; that the Subjects of understanding and the senses might not be trampled under foot by Satan their foe.[2] And may innumerable blessings be upon this Prophet, Ahmad the chosen, and upon his *Sinless Family*.[3]

---

1 This phrase commences every chapter of the Koran except one, and is always used at the beginning of a book. Rahman and Rahino are both adjectives from the same root; but in the meaning there is a shade of difference. For ample information concerning the phrase vide. Lane's Ar. Nights vol 1 p 16 The Bo. 28 of the Nisab-us-sibyan p 1 Sale's Koran Sect 3 of Prelim. Dis. But observe that the usual way of translating both words by "*most merciful*" is culpably careless; although even Golins has explained them by "admodum misericors."

2 This truly Oriental sentence merely means, that God is to be praised for having vouchsafed to man intellect and genius, together with wisdom and learning, to defend his heart from the snares of the devil. The idiom is Persian, and in such phrases as, the diadem of intellect, the steed of genius, the reins of wisdom etc., intellect, genius and wisdom are compared to a crown, a horse, a bridle, etc., etc.

3 It is a well known tenet of almost all Moslems that the tan- i pak, or the five pure persons, viz 1. Mohammed. 2, Ali. 3, Fatimeh. 4, Hasan. 5, Hussin; were holy and without sin—. The Shiahs extend this to their other 9 Imams. From the omission of the

Know, O learned reader! that in the Sanscrit tongue, this book is called Hitopadesa,[4] or "Salutary" "advice", and it contains four chapters, the first of which discusses the subject of friendship, the second treats of the separation of friends, the third touches upon warlike affairs, and teaches us how best to secure victory and to overcome our foe, whereas the fourth gives an account of union, effected either before or after actual fighting. In a word, the chapters contain such curious and wonderful tales, that the hearing and perusal of them are well calculated to render a man most acute in worldly matters, and more over to endow him with the power of discriminating between good and evil deeds.

And for this reason it was that when H.M. Nasir-un-din, who governed the Province of Behar, heard the book (read to him), delighted with the entertaining nature of the stories, the excellence of the advice, the beauty of the subject, and the profitable nature of the tale, he was pleased to direct that someone of his servants would translate it into easy Persian for his private perusal and advantage. One individual executed the order and named the version *Mufarrih-ul-Kulub*.[5] The present Translator, Mir Bahadur Ali-i-Husaini in A.D. 1802 & A.H. 1217, by order of his benefactor, John Gilchrist Esq (long may he live and prosper!) turned the book into easy and current *Hindustani*,[6] such as is used in

---

usual blessing upon the Ashab, or companions of the Prophet, viz. Abu-bakr, Omar and Usman, it would appear that the author was a Shiah.

The word Ahmad is the comparative of Hamid praiseworthy, and Muhammed is the 2nd part. Pass. Of the same triliteral Hebi. Chald. And Arab. Verb Namada, laudavit, laudem promerilt ab aliis. Hence the Moslems apply to their Prophet the promises of the comforter reading periclytos for Paracletos.

Vide Gibbon's Decl & Fall. Chapt 50.

4 Vide Appendix.

5 The exhilarator of Hearts—Mujarrih is also the name of a certain medicine in which rubies, pearls and other precious stones are introduced.

6 Rekhtah, literally the "scattered," is one of the names of the Urdu, or Courtly dialect of India called by us the Moors (after the Portuguese), and Hindustani. It has obtained

conversation by all, high and low, and named it Akhlak-i-Hindi, or the Ethicks of India. All may be assured that whoever will act according to its precepts, will find his heart and *head*[7] cheered by the perfume of intellect, and by increasing his stock of knowledge, will materially tend to promote his comfort and happiness.

End.

---

the name of "scattered" from its being a mixed language of Sanscrit, Hindi, Arabic and Persian.

7 The word damagh here translated "head" literally sig. the brain, the sensorium. It is Pers. and synonymous with the Arab. Mastram in the phrase used in the text.

Akhlak-i-Hindi

or

The Ethicks of India

Introduction to the First Chapter

The story begins as follows. Upon the banks of the Ganges in India, there was a city called *Manikpur*,[8] and the Raja of that place was one *Chandra-Sain*,[9] who had power and dominion over all his caste-fellows. One day as he occupied the Royal throne, his sons *were standing disrespectfully in his presence*.[10] Seeing this want of decorum in them, a person exclaimed "verily without *knowledge*[11] a man is blind, although his eyes may see! Moreover

---

8 In Hind. Manik is a ruby from the S माणिक्य The Affix-pur or -pur which follows the names of so many cities in India is from the S पुर a town.*

*   The Rev S Lee in his transl of Tbn Batuta's travels p 187 in a note upon the word Manikam , says that it is "most likely a Sanscrit word, although we do not find it in Mr Wilson's Sanscrit Dict." It is found in the 2nd edition Calcutta 1832, and the word commonly occurs in Bengali, Hindustani, Mahratta, Guzerati, and other dialects.

One Manikpur is mentioned in Tbn Batuta's travels under the name of Manikbur —Rennell spells it Manicpoor.

9 The word Chandra (S चंद्र) means the moon, and it is often used as part of the name by the Chandra-bausi family of Rajputs, who claim descent from the moon. Sain often occurs as a termination to Hindoo names in Sindh as well as in India.

10 The Son in the East scarcely even sits in the presence of his father; here the sentence merely means that the young men were behaving disrespectfully.

11 The Arab. word ilm which I have here translated knowledge may also sig. science, wisdom, or a branch of study. The whole of this panegyric on wisdom is completely in the Oriental style, and the sentiments would bear a literal translation into Hebrew,

knowledge is the thing, by the might of which all difficulties are solved, and he only is really opulent who possesses that treasure; for neither thieves can steal it, nor any one claim it, nor man discover where it lies. Besides, the more you choose to impart it to others, the greater it becomes, and can by no means diminish. And knowledge is a price-less jewel, a manly ornament, a friend who cleaves to us at home and abroad. Whoever possesses it will be admitted into the society of monarchs, and the intimacy of the great. And of all sciences two are best, wisdom and military knowledge; yet of the two, the former merits our preference. For it suits every one equally; if a child have learning all will bless him, and if an old man possess it, people will open their ears and hearts to his words, and store up his instruction in their memories. Whereas on the contrary if an old man use the sword, the world will deride him saying lo! his wits have taken leave of him in his old age! Be not then slow to get wisdom, nor say in your hearts, why labour and toil so much for this life? Believe me, if you will only acquire knowledge it will so enable you to serve your Creator, that the riches both of this world and of the next will be yours in plenty. Allow not carelessness to delude your hearts with the idea, that you are now young and that many days remain for devotion which ye can then practise at your ease, but that the present is the hour for worldly matters. Rather recollect that Death[12] always grasps the *hair of your heads*,[13] and only awaits the Deity's order instantly to stop your breath, which he will do without allowing you one moment's delay. O my friends! teach your children wisdom in their tender years, and it will abide in their hearts, *like an engraving in stone*;[14] as you see the potters vase

---

Sanscrit, Arabic or Persian. The Prov. of Solomon especially the 4th chapter offer many examples of such exhortation.

12 Once for all I must remark that most of the ideas, allusions and quotations in this book are Moslem not Hindu. Here Azrail or the angel of death is alluded to.

13 The choti (S चूटी) is the lock of hair left on the top of the head, by almost all castes of Hindus and some Mussalman nations.

14 This is an Arabic phrase, more generally written K-an nakshi fi l hajar. For the same sentiment, see Prov. 22. 6.

which, ornamented when in a plastic state, will ever retain the same appearance after it is baked."

The Raja's heart was troubled when he heard these truths, and he hung down his head in grief. Presently he began, "Alas! there are four qualities collected in my sons, namely, youth, wealth, pride and ignorance;—any one of which is sufficient to bring a man to ruin and *utter confusion*.[15] How much better than the child who has not knowledge, or will not act according to its dictates, is the patient ox who carries his burden, and thus greatly benefits mankind—Recollect, when in any meeting men discuss the merits of individuals, only such as are of good repute are called worthy and dutiful children. The parents of those who are badly spoken of, shall be termed barren and childless: It has been said that the Almighty blesses those whom he loves with facility of attaining the six following things. In the first place, daily increase of wisdom. Secondly, good health. Thirdly a good, faithful, and *sweet-spoken*[16] wife. Fourthly, generosity, and fear of the Lord—Fifthly, long life and happiness. Sixthly, some art or profession which may keep him from actual want."

Presently one of the assembly thus addressed the monarch: O Raja! four things are not brought by children from their mother's womb;- good or bad fortune,—wealth or poverty,—knowledge or ignorance,—length or shortness of days. The Almighty has, I hope, destined your sons to be great and wise. Why do you not seek that remedy, which can heal the wounds of your bleeding heart[17] and restore you to perfect moral health?" The Monarch asked to what

---

15 In the original, tin terah, literally *three and thirteen*, as we say "sixes and sevens"—and the Persians shash o panj (sixes and fives.)

16 This is one of the qualities to which Orientals attach much importance. A Persian poet says, "Enter not the walls of that house, outside which the *voice of woman* is heard." In those parts of Asia where the rules of the Harem are strictly kept, it is considered disgraceful for the female inmates to be heard outside the Seraglio. In this point many Christian countries might read a profitable lesson from the Moslem book.

17 Literally "why do you not take the medicine which can remove the thought that turns your heart's blood into water?" A phrase expressive of anxiety and biting care.

remedy he alluded. He replied, "to the *Word of God*[18] which says, "that which I will, I do, without failure and without delay." The Raja answered, "thou hast spoken truly, my friend, but the same Creator gave us hands and feet, senses and hearing, intellect and discernment,—in fact everything requisite, and He enjoined us to get understanding, as well as to be constant in worshipping him. For he is the grantor of human desires, and allows not the labour of those who seek knowledge, to be spent in vain. But he will not do this without some exertion on our part. The clay in the potter's house becomes not a vase by itself, till he kneads it with water, places it upon the wheel, and fashions it with his hands."

Again the Raja enquired whether among those present there was any wise and learned man, able to instruct the young Princes in the arts and sciences, and capable of turning them from the ways of evil into the right road. He quoted the well known proverb, that whatever tree grows near the *Sandal*,[19] it also acquires the peculiarity of Sandals;

For where the Sandal tree expands its branches to the breeze,
It lends its strong and perfumed smell to all the neighbouring trees.

and concludes by observing, that the ignorant by frequenting the assemblies of the wise, may become wise themselves.

A Brahman called *Bishan Sarma*[20] who was seated amongst the company,

---

18 "The Word of God" is the Koran, and in Arab. and Pers. any quotation from its pages is invariably prefaced with Kal Allah—God said. It is one of the orthodox tenets, that the words of the Koran were literally spoken by the Deity, and there fore one of His Sufat or attributes, is Ka-il or Speaking. The quotation appears to be from the Koran, Chapter 36, and it is very slightly altered. The original is, "His command, when he willith a thing, is only that he saith unto it Be; and it is."

19 The sandal tree is a native of the India islands, where as Crawfurd informs us (vol 1, p 519) it is called Aikamenil, Ayasru and Chandana. The latter word is pure Sanscrit (चन्दन) S.M.N. In Arabic it became Sandal and thus found its way into the languages of the West.

20 Bishan, (S विष्णु) corr, form of Vishni, or the Preserving Deity's name. The word Sarma has no meaning, but Sharmma in Sanscrit (शर्मा) is a name or appellation common to Brahmans. Vide. Wilson's Sanscrit Deity sub vocs.

exclaimed, "O great King![21] I can extracate your sons from the whirlpool of ignorance, and seat them in the vessel of *learning*.[22] For by labour even a bird may be made to speak,—much more these youths who are the sons of a Raja.[23] With God's aid in the space of six months, I will impart to them the knowledge they require." The monarch was delighted at this, and uttered the following words, "if insects will remain in flowers, they will by virtue of the latter, be carried upon the heads of the great. So also, if my sons abide in your Service, their present *load*[24] of ignorance will certainly be exchanged for the precious burden of knowledge." Having thus commended the Brahman, the raja committed his sons to his care. Bishan Sarma took the youths by the hand, and leading them to this own house, began to advise them in the following words. "Hear, O Princes! The hours of the wise are spent in reading, writing and acquiring knowledge,—in such occupations their joy lies. But fools pass their days and nights in foolish talking and the slumbers of carelessness or in gossipping and quarrelling with their neighbours,—such are their delights. Now for your benefit I will relate some tales of certain very loving friends, the Crow, the Tortoise, the Deer and the Mouse, in the form of apologues, by hearing which man's intellect is brightened and his understanding increased." The Princes replied, "proceed, sit we listen to you with heart and soul."

In is difficult to imagine how this name can have been changed into Bidpai in Persian. Bi'dba' in Arabic and Pilpay in the Languages of the West; unless we suppose that the original Translator's thought is sufficient to preserve the sentiments of the Indian work, without retaining the names of persons and places. Moreover no Arab or Persian could pronounce *Vishnu* properly, more Indico.

21 Maha'raj literally signifies "great King", but it is popularly used in addressing any superior, and also to an inferior, ironically.

22 Ignorance, being a fatal snare, is compared to a whirlpool; whereas knowledge or wisdom which is a man's safeguard, is likened to a ship.

23 "Labor improbus omnia vincit."

24 The word Hasho here translated "load," literally signifies, any coarse and cheap article, with which pillows, cushions etc., are stuffed and the sentence runs thus in the original, "the stuffing of want of understanding, now collected in their breasts shall be removed, and replaced by the jewel of knowledge."

Chapter 1
Mitra labha[25] or the Tale of Lakh-Patank[1] the Crow, illustrating the mutual Advantage to be derived from Friendship.

Bishan Sarma the *Pandit*[26] thus began, "I am now going to treat of the meeting of friends, and to show you how men who are powerless and wise, poor and united by friendship, manage to get on in the world like the four animals in my story." The Princes asked how that might be, and begged their instructor to explain it all to them in detail. The Pandit said. On the banks of the *Godavery River*[27] was a large *sambal*[28] tree, on whose boughs all the birds of that neighbourhood were wont to roost. One morning, before daylight

---

25 Mitra-labha, or "the acquisition of a friend," is the title of the First Chapter of the Sanscrit Hito—padesa. Mitra, s.m. a friend, the sun, (whence the name of the Persian deity, "Mithras," and the old Persian word mihr, love.) Labha s.m. acquirement, acquisition. The title of this chapter in the Guzeratti version, is *mitra-prapti* and signifies the same thing as mitra-labha. In the Mahratta translation, it is *su-hreul-labha* from su-hreud, a friend, and labha—I have written the name of the Crow, "*Lakh Patank*," because it is always pronounced so; but in the Sanscrit it is (लघु पटनक) Laghu-Patanak,— "the *light* or *active* bird," from laghu adj. light, nimble, and patan, s.m. a bird, (from the root pat. to go, move.) In this chapter, the Hindoo Mentor explains to his pupils, the way of making friends for themselves, and Lakh-Patank, the crow who wanders about in search of a friend, is proposed to them as a model.

26 Pandit. (S पंडित) s.m. a scholar, learned Brahman from Pand. (S पाण्ड) s.m.n. wisdom, science learning.

27 In the Hitopadisa, the scene of this tale is laid upon the banks of the Godavery—a River in the Peninsula.

28 In Hind. Sambal or Semal. in Sanscr. (शात्मलि) shatmali. s.m.f. the Bombay heptaphy Uum, or silk cotton tree.

appeared, Lakh-Patank the crow, on opening his eyes *beheld to his astonishment*[29] a fowler walking along with his net upon his shoulder, and having very much the look of an Angel of Death. The bird became thoughtful and remarked to himself, *"this is certainly an ill-omened sight to begin the day with,*[30] I must see what it portends." Thus saying he followed the fowler a short way, till at last he saw him draw forth some rice from his bag, scatter it upon a spot under a tree, spread the net which he carried on his shoulders over it, and hide himself in a corner. At this very moment, the king of the Pigeons, by name *Chitra-Griv*[31] accompanied by his host, alighted from the air on that same place, and several of the pigeons happened to espy the scattered grain. Every one was seized with a desire to devour it, but Chitra-Griv seeing his dependants thus foolishly entertaining vain desires, said to them, "my friends! only reflect a little. In the jungle where we now are, whence could the grain have come? Were this an inhabited spot, you might say that this rice might have fallen upon the ground whilst men were at their meals[32] but here such is not the case, and what you see under this tree is certainly not without some deceit. Should you descend for

---

29   This kind of question in Hindustani "what does he see?" is an idiomatic form of expressing the bird's wonder and astonishment at seeing the object afterwards named, and thus I have translated it throughout this version.

30   Throughout Asia there is no more common idea than that the first words uttered, and the first object seen, in the morning, portend good or evil throughout the day. The natives therefore are careful that their words on awaking from sleep should be of a propitious nature, and a Mussleman usually utters some pious ejaculations as ya hu O God!. The objects most lucky to be seen on first rising are sometimes very whimsically chosen, as e.p.a. baboon.

31   A compound Sanscrit name, "spotted neck"; from Chitra adj. Spotted, variegated. Griva s.f. the neck, the nape.
       This story of the pigeons teaches the necessity of prudence, the duties of a Prince to his subjects, the power of unanimity, and the advantages of friendship in the hour of need.

32   This use of the active and casual verb gives a peculiar naivete to the sentence, but as is generally the case with such idioms, is utterly beyond the reach of translation.

the purpose of eating it, your fate will be very similar to that of the traveller, who for the sake of a golden *anklet*[33] stuck in the quagmire, and became the old Tiger of prey." The Pigeons enquired what that might be—Chitra-Griv thus related to them . . .

---

33 Payal S.S J. an ornament for the ankle. The Hitopadesa has kankan s.m.n. a bracelet. The following tale shows the folly of expecting good from the bad, and warns us never to trust to our natural enemies,—a favourite theme in Oriental advice.

The Story of the old Tiger and the Traveller.

One day, I had gone out to feed in a certain jungle in the Deccan, and there saw an old tiger, *with his face turned towards the Caaba,*[34] sitting upon the side of a tank, in an attitude of great humility. Whenever a traveller or wayfarer passed along that road, he made a point of informing him, that he had a golden anklet, which he desired to give away *in charity*[35] and would present it to any one who would receive it. But no one dared approach him. One day it so happened that a traveller, *guided by* fate[36] felt violently desirous of getting that jewel from the tiger.[37] He reflected that so precious an article was not to be had gratis every day, and was convinced that on this occasion his good fortune had aided, and his fate assisted him. Full of these ideas, he thought of going up to the tiger, but again bodily fear suggested that it would be folly at once to trust to the sugared words of a foe; that although the tiger had the anklet by him, yet how was it to be taken from him?—that poison is not the less fatal because mixed up with honey, and that the good in which evil also dwells is not much to be coveted. On the other hand desire reminded him, that "where

---

34 In all countries Moslems pray with their faces turned towards the Caaba, or House of God at Mecca. The old tiger here would persuade the traveller that he is engaged in holy contemplation etc. For full information concerning the Caaba, vide Crichton's Hist. of Arab. vol 1, cap 3, & vol 2 cap 5. Sales' Koran. Prel. Dis. Sect. 1 et passim. D'Herbelot. Bibl. Orient. sub voce Caaba.

35 Lit "On the way of God." a lit. translation of the Arab. Phrase fi sabil illah, and meaning alms given to travellers, beggars etc. on the *road* or sabil.

36 Literally "seized by sudden or predestined death"—and meaning that his term of life being now expired, fate had claimed him.

37 The word Sher is Persian and in that language never means anything but a lion, as in Arabic. Asad. In Hind. it is used for either tiger or lion.

the hoard is there too the snake lies, where the rose is, there too is the thorn."[38] That danger exists everywhere for one in want of money that if through fear this opportunity be suffered to pass, another might never present itself and that many and grievous toils and hardships must be endured by men before they become rich.

After much and serious thought, he at length asked the tiger to let him see the article which he desired to give away in charity. The animal stretched out his paw, and showed him the anklet. The traveller said, "thou are a tiger, I am a man; consequently my body is thy prey. On thee I can have no reliance, and therefore cannot come within my reach." "Knowest thou not," said the tiger, "that I have *left off eating* animal food?[39] If I desired flesh, could I not speedily satisfy myself with some venison out of the jungle; or why should I not seize and devour thee? But no, I have made a vow of abstinence. Now this anklet is of no use to me—seeing thy poverty, I desire to *merit reward in Heaven*[40] by giving it to thee. Never fear me man! Approach without dread! I value the lives of others, as much as I do my own! "But how was it," said the wayfarer, "that thou hast not given it to any one of those who passed by this road?" The tiger replied, "it is of little use to give to the wealthy—Medicine is for the sick, not the robust and healthy, and glory in Heaven awaits those who feed the poor." Those words completely deceived the traveller who exclaimed, "0 good natured

---

38 The idea that hoards and hidden treasures are defended by evil spirits, ghosts, dragons and snakes is too well known both in the West and the East to require explanation.

39 Some sects of Moslems, as for instance the Sufis, greatly commend abstaining from animal food in general, eating little, and a particular kind of discipline called Kiyazat, which is a fast of so rigid a nature that it generally all but kills the patient. Orthodox Moslems say that these opinions were borrowed from the Hindoos, and the Shiahs declare that they were invented in the time of the Abbasides, in order to detract from the merit of their Imams.

40 It is the remark of my old teacher, Moonshee Dossabhai Sohrabje that the English language has no word which singly expresses the meaning of the Arabic "Sawab."

animal! give me the anklet." The tiger directed him *first to bathe*[41] in the tank, and then to draw nigh. The wretch in joyful anticipation of receiving the jewel, hurried into the water, and found both his feet stuck in quagmire. His foe perceived that the prey was securely entrapped, and arising advanced very slowly to seize it." Where are thou coming O Tiger?" asked the man. "Merely to extracate thee from the mud," replied the beast. No sooner had he uttered these words than he seized the traveller's neck. During the operation, the latter cursed his own folly again and again, and cried out "Alas! Alas! If you sprinkle the bitter pumpkin's root with sherbet instead of water yet will its fruit be bitter as gall."

A man's own nature ne'er can change, what e'en that nature be,
As him trees bitter will remain, though fed with goor and ghee.[42]

"Although to excite cupidity in my unhappy heart, he uttered some sugared words, yet at last his natural ferocity showed itself. Had his nature been good, evil could never have proceeded from it, and his actions could not have been such. So when the cow eats *dry grass and gives sweet milk,*[43] her milk is sweet, not by reason of the grass, but because it is her nature to produce such." These were the travellers last words, and thus, O my brethren! if you alight under the

---

41 Lest being impure from accidental cause he might touch the tiger and thus communicate the impurity to him. For after wuzoo or ghusl (the two forms of ablution) between that and prayer if touched by anything impure, the ablution has to be repeated.

42 This bait or distich is in the Braj Bhakha, and well known in India. The him or Nimb tree (Melia Azedirachta) has most bitter leaves and bark. The former are eaten by some natives as an antidote against the poison of snakes, and the twigs are used for dautans, or tooth brushes.

43 Our author's explanation of this phenomenan is far more philosophical than that offered by our old authors as the following quotation will prove. "Q. Why is milk white seeing the flowers are red which it is engendered of?"—A. Because every humour which is engendered of the body is made like unto that part in colour where it is engendered as near as it can be; but because the flesh of the paps is white, therefore the colour of the milk is white."
    Problems of Alexander Aphrodisiacus.

tree to eat that grain, you will uselessly throw away your lives in your greedi-
ness, even as the foolish wayfarer did for the sake of the anklet. Then indeed
you will appreciate the value of safety, my friend! Under this tree as yet I never
saw grain. The wise have declared that no evil proceeds from the following six
things—moderation in eating, a well educated son, a prudent and submissive
wife, a master bound to us by the tie of gratitude for our services, a word
weighed before uttered, and an action undertaken by the advice of the wise. As
your value your weal, abandon this grain.

One of the pigeons who was the most foolish of the party then said, "Brethren! if we be deterred by such gossip, we might as well give up eating at once.
Wherever we go to feed, if we allow such apprehensions to overcome us, with
our own hands we shut the door, in the face as it were, of our daily bread. I for
one will never leave this grain."

Well, when all the pigeons followed his advice and alighted under the tree,
Chitra-Griv whose prudence and wisdom were such, that to him nothing was
difficult; and whose constant habit it was to counsel and admonish others, when
all his friends had descended, said to himself, "it is very little satisfaction to me
to remain alone. The proverb says death with a crowd is as good as a feast
whatever be the consequences, I will accompany them." So at last he too
descended with them, and became a partner in their imprudence. The fowler
saw that all had now fallen into the snare. He instantly pulled the net, and all
the pigeons found themselves entrapped. Then they began to curse and blame
their silly counsellor, and to attribute their descent from the tree, and capture
in the snare, to his advice. The foolish pigeon, on the other hand, was so much
ashamed when he heard their taunts and reproaches, that he knew not how to
show his face. Presently he exclaimed, "truly said the wise men of old, that it
profits little to an individual who finds himself involved in difficulty with ten
others, to take the lead of them in opposition; for if he succeeds all the rest will
take away from his credit, by declaring that they aided him in succeeding; and
if (which may God avert!) *the event be different,*[44] all will lay the whole blame of

---

44 Amongst Asiatics, as was also the case with the Greeks and Romans, it is considered

the failure at his door." Chitra-Griv told them that this was not the proper time for reproaches. -

Reproof is allowed in the hour of peace,
In the hour of destruction blame should cease.

"Brethren! this error and sin belong to no one, whatever God wills, that and that alone can take place."

The hand of Fate hath fingers five,
Tis vain with it for life to strive;
Two stop the ears, two close the eyes,
One shuts the mouth and lo! man died.

"Friends! In the *evil day*,[45] even good turns into bad, as for instance, the affection of parents for their children, though generally speaking great, occasionally becomes enmity and hatred. We may compare it to this; when the herdsman milks the cow he tethers the calf's neck to its parents leg, at which time the mother's leg becomes her offsprings foe, and that herdsman thereby accomplishes what he desires. Hear, O my friends! Now cease this clamour! Think of some plan which may release us all. He only is a true friend who aids his friends in the hour of need. In prosperity all will call themselves our friends. People

---

inauspicious to mention any ill omened event too plainly—It is therefore generally merely alluded to, or sometimes hinted at by an opposite form of expression. For instance the polite way of ordering a table-cloth to be removed, is to direct the attendants to increase (the table; barhana); for fear that the inauspicious use of the word le- jana should affect the future meals. In speaking of Death, sickness, failure, misfortune and many other occurrences, especially as in any way connected with the person addressed, it is only the uneducated who use the literal words.

45 *"The evil day"* is that of misfortune affecting either an individual or a body of people. Judicial astrology enables men to decide what are favourable moments for any undertaking and an experienced astrologer can always suggest means of avoiding any impending dangers. It is rather extraordinary that almost all Moslems believe in and encourage judicial astrology, although their prophet expressly declared that astrologers were liars.

call him not a man who when a necessary action is to be undertaken by him, allows himself to be cast down. On the contrary, such willever be termed a coward. He only can lay claim to the name of a man who, whatever misfortune befalls him, still preserves his presence of mind, and cooly and determinately meditates upon the best means of extracating himself. The wise of old have said."

Vain are regrets, whate'er the pen[46] of destiny
Assigns to mortals, that, and only that can be.

On this occasion we must take thought of that which may save us all from this bondage. For men of understanding teach us, that there are six things which become a man,—presence of mind in the hour of sudden calamity,—respect and the observance of ceremony in the reception of a superior,—well timed speech in Society,—a good heart in the day of battle,—preserving oneself from the malignant tongues of men so as to be called persons of good report, and finally a determination to acquire knowledge. And six things are unbecoming to man,—much sleep,—laxity in the performance of religious duties,—shrinking from all undertakings,—excess of wrath,—being badly spoken of by our neighbours,—slandering and deriding others behind their backs. Now, O my brethren act in concurrence with me, and hearken unto my words! So shall ye

---

46 The Kilk or Kalam is the pen with which the decrees of the Deity are inscribed upon the lauh-i-mahfur, or the tablet which receives them. Of the word Kalam we may remark that in Sans. (कलम Kalam) is a writing reed. Hence the Ar. Kalam signifying the same thing. Hence the Greek (Kalamos) a reed, and the Latin *Calamus*, a reed, stalk, pen. "Kaza," I have translated "Destiny," but it is quite erroneous to suppose that Islam is a religion of predestination. The Arabian Prophet was most severe in his declamations against predestinarians and called them *"the Magians* (or Infidels,) *of his faith.* See the Hadis at length in the Iazkiratul. Aimmeh Cap. 2. Almost all our ancient ideas of the Mussalman religion are taken from the theory and practice of the Turks, mixed up with a little of that impious bigotry which thundered anathemas against Mohammed's *God,* because it could not understand an Arabic word, and the credulity on Knavery which retailed or invented the calumnies of Mohammed's despoiling orphans, and being the lover of his own daughter. vide Pridlan's Life of Mahomet. Gibbons Decl & Fall Ch. 50 Chrichton's Hist of Arabia. Introduction.

escape this danger." The pigeons said, "0 King! if we had obeyed you at first, this disgrace and approbium would have been spared us. Now, whatever your orders be, we are ready to execute them." The Monarch said,[47] "what has occurred has occurred, but now let all of you unanimously and simultaneously spring into the air with the net. A single blade of grass, for instance, is insufficient so to bind a sparrow, but that he can burst it; a rope when spun with many such will so confine an elephant, that no struggles can release him." In a word, as Chitra-Griv advised, so all the pigeons did—that is to say, they all in a body flew up carrying the net with them by main force. The fowler followed them up for some *Cos*,[48] but when they disappeared, he lost all hopes and returned homewards. The birds now asked their king what they had better do, since the *Shikaree*[49] was now *disappointed in his expectations*[50] of eating their flesh. "My friends," replied Chitra-Griv, "in this world our parents sympathize with us in our pains and troubles because their affection proceeds from the heart; but all others have some private end to serve in seeking our amity—this hour is not the time for such. However a friend of mine, a certain mouse by name *Hirannik*,[51]

---

47 Here a passage has been omitted because it exactly copies one in P. 10. The written style of Hindustani is disfigured by perpetual tautology, and for that reason, unlike the Arabic and Persian it is most unfit for literal translation into the languages of the West. Here the repetition is probably an error of the copyist.

48 In Sansc. (कोश) Krosha s.m. a distance of 4000 or 8000 cubits. The average in India is about 2 miles. In Persian the word becomes Kuruh—(though not now used in that language). In Hindustani, Guzeratti and Mahrattas, Kos or as it is more generally written *Cos*. In Scindee Kuh.

49 This is almost a household word in British India. It signifies a man (generally of particular caste), whose life is passed in the chase.

50 Literally, "has washed his hands of our flesh;" i.e., has abandoned the pursuit of despair.

51 This is the way the word is pronounced in Hindustani, but in Sansc. it is (हिरण्यक) Hiranyaka. fr. Hiranya s.s.n. gold, silver, wealth, either because, as it afterwards appears, the mouse had been very wealthy, or because there is an idea in the last that mice are fond of stealing and hoarding up precious metals. Our word mouse is thus

dwells in the Bichitra Ban upon the banks of the river Gandak. If we can only arrive there he will speedily gnaw through your bonds." Hearing these words the pigeons sought the mouse's burrow. Hirannik, who in his prudence had dug a hundred branches in his subteranneous retreat, perceived their approach and concealed himself. Presently recognising, he came forth and exclaimed, "Oh ho! great is my good fortune, since my beloved Chitra-Griv deigns thus to honour my poor abode!" Then he saw that all the pigeons were entangled in the meshes. Remaining silent for a moment, he presently asked his friend what the matter might be. "What shall I say?"[52] answered Chitra-Griv, "this is the consequences of our sins. With your wisdom why ask such a question?" The mouse replied, "you speak truly; whatever is fated to happen to an individual for any reason, such must inevitably take place, for as much as pain and pleasure, happiness and misery are meted out according to our merits or demerits." So saying he hastened to gnaw the meshes which entangled Chitra-Griv. The latter remarked "this is not right; begin by cutting the knots which confine my friends and then set me free." "My teeth," said the mouse are not very strong,—how shall I be able to gnaw this through all these nooses, and then extracate you from the net?" "In that case," rejoined Chitra-Griv, "first cut their bonds." Hirannik objected that it is not right to save others at the risk of our own lives, that it was a saying of the wise, that men use riches and friends to ward off calamities; that is to say, they save their own lives by means of wealth and dependants, and that one's own existence should be preferred to everything, since, both in a religious and mundane point of view, upon it all depends. "My friend," replied Chitra-Griv, "this is as you say, the way of the world, but I for one cannot bear to see my dependants unhappy. It is a saying of the olden time, that the sage will devote both life and wealth to even a stranger; if then it be right and proper to sacrifice one's riches and existence to such a

---

der. Latin mus; from Greek (mus); from Persian mush; from Sansc. (मूषक) mushaka.

52 This answering a question by a question is a most uncomfortable idiom to a beginner. It denotes however an affirmation here and means that the speaker knows not what to say.

one, how much more am I bound to do this for my friends, who in *caste*[53] and in strength are all my equals? By exalting me to dignity, what advantage can they derive? They remain in my friendship without reward. Rest assured that I am ready to lay down my life, if by this their liberation can be affected. For what reliance can be placed upon the mortal frame? If by means of it any good can be done in this world,—such is indeed a worthy use of it; for our dust may become as nothing in a single moment, whereas the memory of our deeds will survive its wreck for thousands of years."

Hirannik was delighted at hearing these words and said, *"praise be to thee*[54] for that their heart is so devoted to thy friends." Well, the mouse cut all the bonds which confined the pigeon's legs, and paid them all the usual compliments.[55] Then turning towards Chitra Griv, he said to him, "friend do not afflict yourself because you fell into the net, since these toils and troubles, must and will thus causelessly befall us all." "True," said the monarch, but had we been wise, we should not have fallen into the fowler's snare." The mouse replied, "what knows the *vulture*,[56] soaring in the sky, when seeing a bit of flesh upon the ground, he descends towards it whether a trap has been laid for him or not? For the weak intellect of the creature is utterly unable to comprehend, much less to interfere with, the will of the Creator. Such is the might of the evil

---

53 This word so much used in British India, is derived from a source which has supplied us with many garbled names of Eastern things,—the Portuguese. Casta s.f. race, family, species. Hence Mandarim from Mandar to command. Gentoo from Gentio, a heathen. The Moors (Hindustani!) from Maurs, an inhabitant of Mauritania in Northern Africa; and though the following derivation is merely a guess, I think we may trace Pagoda to Pagao, a Pagan.

54 Literally, "a hundred bravos to thee."

55 They being his guests.

56 The "Kargas" is one of the numerous fabulous birds of Persian story, and is supposed to be enamoured of flesh. It is gen. translated the vulture. For other fabulous birds see in the Dictionaries under, Anka, Huma, Rukh (Rukhkh), Keekness, Sirang, Simurgh, Sirnas. The Kargo may be derived from the Sansc. (खगेश) Khagesh, (literally, the lord of birds) the adjutant bird.

Day, that not even the sun and moon can defend themselves from *eclipse*."[57]
After these few words of advice and comfort, Hirannik performed the rites of
hospitality to his visitors, and bade them farewell. The two friends, with brimming
eyes, affectionately embraced, and the mouse quoted these lines of Sheikh Saadi.[58]

> *The heart and eyes of Saadi are with thee on thy way,*
> *Think not thou goest forth alone, though far and far away.*

Chitra-Griv, the King of the pigeons, together with his army turned towards
his own country, and Hirannik crept into his burrow. On the other hand Lakh
Patank that same crow, who, as has before been related, saw the fowler so early
in the morning and followed up the search of adventure, was struck with astonishment on seeing what had occurred to the pigeons. *"Praise be to God,"*![59]
said he, "see how vast are the advantages of affection and friendship, and what
use a friend may prove himself in the hour of adversity"!

---

57   The Hindus believe that eclipses are caused by the efforts of the demon Rahu to
     wreak vengeance on the sun and moon. See Moors Pantheon P. 283. Even the Mos-
     lems think the Kusuf and Khusuf, or eclipses of the sun and moon, times of calamity
     and have certain prayers for them. The word gahan or grahan is also idiomatically
     applied to a hated ruler, and if an officer who is much disliked, die or be removed
     from a place, the Seapoy will often congratulate his comrade that "the eclipse has left
     his head." In astrology an eclipse of the sun forebodes evil to Monarchs and such, an
     eclipse of the moon to Ministers, Vazirs, etc.

58   Sheikh Muslihud-din Saadi, born at Ahiraz A.H. 571 a celebrated author in prose and
     verse in Arabic as well as in Persian. His chief works are the Gulistan, the Bustan,
     Ghazals (odis) Kasidehs (short poems) and Mutayyibat or pleasantries. He was a
     Sunni and a Dervaysh, was several times married, and all his wives turned out badly.
     Of his children, only one daughter is mentioned. She was almost her father's equal in
     wit. Saadi died in A.H. 691, others say sooner, and was buried near Shiraz. His tomb
     called Saadiyeh still exists. He is not much respected in a religious point of view by
     his countrymen at present, who are Shiahs, but Sunnis and Sufis look up to him with
     the greatest reverence. Hence he is always called Sheikh (or as here Makhdum) Saadi.

59   An interjection, used in sign of admiration, astonishment, wonder, etc., etc.

The elephant [60] *stuck in the mire,*
Strong elephants only can extracate,
And truest friends only can save,
A friend from the torrent of adverse fate.

The crow then approached the mouse's burrow, and in a low soft voice began to say, "A Hirannik! I have travelled far, but in all my wanderings throughout the world, I never beheld so faithful a friend as you are. I have a favour to ask of you, if you will grant it, I will say what it is." When the mouse heard the crow's voice, he cried out from his hole, "who are thou, and whence comest thou?" The other replied, "I am a crow by name Lakh Patank, and now my desire is to become one of your friends." Hirannik said, "I am a mouse, thou are a crow, I therefore am thy food and thou an habitual eater of my kind. How then is it possible that friendship can subsist between us? Go, and engage in intimacy with some crow, or some other such bird. If I become thy friend, our story may be very much like that of the jackal and the deer's friendship." The crow enquired what that might be, and the mouse thus proceeded with the tale of . . .

---

60 A common Sanscrit name for the elephant, is (पीलु) Pilu. This in old Persian became pil, and as the Arabians must first have seen the animal in that country, but have no letter (p) in their alphabet they altered the name to fil. This with the article would be el-fil. In Greek the word becomes (elephas), and in Latin, Elphas and Elephantus. But the learned Parkhurst chooses to derive elephant from the Hebrew Aleph, *because* that word signifies "bos" and Pliny and Vairo tell us that when the Romans first saw elephants in Lucania, they called them "Lucas Boves," or Lucanian oxen! When we can trace the word through the Greek and Persian languages to their common parent the Sanscrit, it is surely unnecessary to deviate into Hebrew.

So also in the case of the word *"pepper"* In Sanscrit it is (पिपलि) pippili; in Arabic for the reason above given it becomes filfil—in Greek (peperi) in Latin Piper, and hence it has descended to the languages of modern Europe. Yet a Greek or Latin dictionary, will *generally* derive the word a (pepeiros, maturus,) quod suo coctionem juvet.

The Crow, the Deer and the Jackal.

I have been told that in Eastern India, upon the banks of the Ganges, there is a town called Champawati, and that in a jungle somewhere near it, a crow and a deer, two intimate friends were in the habit of residing. Now the latter of these was so stout and well looking, that a certain jackal, seeing his condition became highly delighted and resolved in his heart to try some of his fool's tricks with the deer, and finally to *destroy and devour*[61] him if possible. With this intention he very gently advanced towards the antelope and said, "*As's alamo alayk!*[62] are you hale and well?" The other asked him who he was; he replied, "I am a jackal by name *Chhudra-budh*[63] and thus living in this jungle without a friend, I am more dead than alive. Now that I have met with you, I can number myself amongst the living, and feel that life once more animates this frame." Whilst this conversation was going on, the white *goose*[64] had flown

---

61 Lit. "Warm my grinders with his meat." This tale is intended to show the danger of entrusting our secrets to a stranger, and the necessity of being upon our guard, in our dealings with those whom we know not.

62 The proper Moslem salutation, "peace be unto you;" used with certain modifications all throughout the East; but what is rather extraordinary, it is less common in Arabia than probably anywhere else. The Arab's salutation is Sabbahk allah (or Massak allah) bi'l Khair,—good morning, or good evening to thee.

63 Chhudra s. adj. (शुद्र) Kahudra—low, mean, and   Budh s.s.f. (बुद्धि) buddhi, intellect, understanding—So al so su S. adj. (सु) good, excellent, and budh—(the Crow's name.)

64 This sentence is a poor imitation of the figurative Persian style. The Sun, being of a brilliant colour, is compared to a goose; the heavens to an azure lake, in which the sun is swimming; the bank denotes the visible horizon, and the falcon being a dark coloured bird at enmity with the Kaz, represents the night. The whole phrase signifies that it became dark. In Persian these rhetorical flourishes are constantly occurring, and some are extremely difficult to the beginner. But all who desire to be intimately

from the azure sea, and landing upon the bank had plunged behind it; when presently the black falcon of night became visible. The deer retired to his usual sleeping place, and the jackal also followed him up as far as his abode. In that place was a *Champaca*[65] tree, the abode of a certain crow by name Su-budh, an old friend of the deer's. He instantly asked the latter, friend! who may this stranger be?—that you have thus brought him with you." "This," said the deer, "is a jackal, he appears to be a worthy kind of animal, and desires to become a friend of mine." His friend replied, "when you are not acquainted with an individual it is not right at once to rely upon his words, but above all things you ought never to show him your home. But have you really never heard the tale of that vulture and the cat?" The deer asked what it might be, and the crow thus began . . .

acquainted with the language cannot attend too much to these phrases. I have translated Kaz, a goose, and so the Dictionaries give it, but am not sure that it does not mean a kind of white crane, with which a peculiar breed of falcon (called shahin) is taught to fight. In all Eastern dialects there is a great confusion in the names of birds, trees, plants, etc.

65 Champa, in Hind. Champaka in Sansc. the tree Michelia Champaca which bears a yellow flower, much admired by the Hindoos.

The Story of the old Vulture and the Cat.

I have been told that upon the banks of the River Bhagirathi,[66] there is a lofty hill which they call *Gird-kot*,[67] upon which was a large Sembal-tree,[68] in whose hollow trunk an old decrepid vulture had dwelt for many years. His wings and feathers no longer retained the power of carrying him here and there in search of food; but most of the birds whose homes were in that tree used to bring home some food for him in their beaks, and thus he was accustomed to pass his days. On one occasion a certain cat approached the spot, with the view of devouring the offspring of its inhabitants. No sooner did the young birds see her, then they instantly began to utter loud cries; but the vulture, being blind through old age, could not distinguish anything. Startled however by the clamour, he put out his head and asked who it was, that had ventured to intrude. The cat was much terrified when she saw his formidable appearance, and said in her heart, "I am done for now, as there is no way of escape; better then approach him, and concoct some story by which his mind may be deceived." So very slowly drawing near the vulture, she salaamed to him. He asked who it was. With great humility she replied, "I am a wretched cat." "A Cat!" said the vulture; "if so, you had better leave this place with all possible speed, otherwise, as I am hungry, I will instantly drink up your blood." "Permit me," replied she, "to make but one remark, and then if you think me wor

---

66 A classical name of the River Ganges—for the derivation of which Vid Moor's Pantheon P. 339.

  This story again is a warning against strangers, and putting confidence in those with whom we are not most intimately acquainted.

67 The Sansc. Hitopadesa gives this word (गृध्रकूट) grendha-kut literally the "vulture's dwelling," peak, or summit. Why it should have been altered into Gird-kot, I cannot say.

68 Vide Appendix. In the Sansc. however the tree is called a (प्रक्कटि) parkkati s.f. waved-leaf fig tree.

thy of destruction, slay me—otherwise allow me to depart." The vulture said "explain whatever may be in your heart." Hear me, Sir proceeded the Cat, "the good and the bad are known by their words and deeds. It is very truly and generally asserted that the feline species is both murderous and carnivorous, and if under this idea you put me to death, you *will show your greatness*.[69] But perhaps no one has informed you of my *abstinence and devotion*;[70] that I do nothing without previous ablution, and have utterly left off eating the flesh of animals; that I value the lives of others as much as I prize my own, and pass my days and nights in the service of the Almighty. The humble individual who now stands before you, has often heard the birds who flock from this tree to feed upon the banks of the Ganges expatiate upon your virtues, and in her sinful heart became extremely desirous of *waiting upon*[71] one so holy, that her sins might thereby be forgiven her. With this intention she has *ventured into your presence*[2] and you design her destruction. This is an action which no one but yourself ever thought of. When the woodcutter takes up his axe, and sets out with the intention of cutting down trees, the tree under which he is seated, for its own honour removes not its *shade*[72] from his head. All this distance have I travelled for the purpose of seeing you, and now you desire to put me to death! If a guest enter another's abode, and the master of the house does not

---

69 Meaning that she would not prevent it.

70 See D'Herbetot Bibl. Orient. under the words Zohd and Zahed; and for penances, see Herktot's Qanoon i Islam P. 301. In reading the latter volume however it must be recollected that however faithful be the portrait which it offers of Islam in India, it no more describes the customs of true Mohammedanism, than an account of the life of an Abyssinian Christian would explain the tenets of Christianity.

71 & 2 Literally, "see your feet"; a phrase of great humility, implying that the speaker deserves not to look at the face of the person he addresses. And in general when addressing one much superior to oneself, "*his feet*" are used for "*himself*."

72 Here it may be as well to explain the common Oriental phrase, "may your shadow never be less." It means, may the shade which you cast upon my head or the protection which you afford me, never be withdrawn from me. See P. 57 note 130.

entertain him, still he uses not the bitter words which you have addressed to me. Although he may not show him overmuch courtesy, still he at least offers him a draught of cold water and uses kind languages. In compassionate and good hearted treat with equal attention all who come to them, whether learned or ignorant, as the sun which debard none from its light, and does not illuminate the palace of the rich man, whilst it leaves the poor mans cottage in darkness."[73]

When the vulture's heart was melted by these words he said, "upon this tree certain birds have left their young; it was for precautions sake that I said that much to you,—dismiss the thing from your mind." "Astaghfirn'llah"[74] cried the cat, placing both paws upon her ears, "had anyone but you issued those words, I should have *poisoned myself,*[75] in consequence. I have passed many books upon the subject of learning,[76] and know right well the path to heaven. The wise, the virtuous and the religious have told me that to afflict another heart, is one of the *mortal sins.*[77]

---

73 This comparison is natural and touching. It is a great favourite with the Hindoo poets, etc.; though the moon's light is generally introduced instead of the sun's.

74 Literally, "I intreat forgiveness of God!" an expression very often used when wishing to disclaim anything with which one may be charged. Placing the hands to the ears is a sign of horror at what has just been said.

75 For then the crime would lie at the vulture's door. This threat, as used for purposes of extorting gifts, alms, etc., from an unwilling donor, is more common amongst Hindoos than Moslems; though occasionally practised by the latter.

76 That is to say, "religious learning," consisting of a knowledge of the Koran. Hadis (or traditions) and the sciences connected with his faith,—the only learning a good Mussalman cares for.

77 The mortal sin, (kabirch opposed to saghireh, or venial offences) as enumerated in the catechism called Tohfat-ul-Ashab, by Murza Abdul-Azim are 7 in number—1. Idolatry. 2 murder. 3, Adultery, 4. Devouring the orphan's substance, 5. Fornication and all impurity, 6. Leaving the field of battle, when an Imam leads to a Crusade or holy war. 7, disobedience towards parents. The sentiment in the text may appear over strained but it is held by all Dervishes, Sufis and many other sets of Moslems. Saadi says in the Bustan,

Whoever slaughters and devours an animal, enjoys the flavour of the same merely as long as it passes over his tongue; no sooner does it pass down his throat, than all is gone. (For this short moment of pleasure), he never considers that his hapless victim has lost its life, and the agony which it endured as that life departed. Now what pleasure can there be in eating such things? knows not the eater that *to-morrow*[78] he will have to answer for all this,—and does he ever reflect how he will succeed in doing so? Verily with his own eyes he shall see the punishment of paining animals, and of taking the life of even an ant. He should therefore value the ant's existence more than his own, for Death cannot be escaped, but doing evil should be avoided as much as possible."

By these deceitful words of the cat, the vulture's heart was quite softened. In a word after the above dialogue the cat took up her abode in the tree,—and after having remained there for a day or two, the deceitful wretch went very

---

Be-ihsanasudeh Kardan dil-i.
Beh ar alf ruk'at be har manzil-i
That to joy one heart by the kindness

Is better than a thousand Rukats (or bowing in prayer) at every stage—and that moralists even extends his principle to not afflicting animals, as we find in the same work.

Mayazar mur-i kih daneh-kash ast
Kih jan darad o jan-i-shirin Kh'ash ast.
Annoy not the little ant, which draws along its grain of corn
For it possesses existence, and existence is sweet and dear to all.

78 *"To-morrow"* denotes the day of resurrection or judgment, (Kiyamat) and is so called on account of its certainty and comparative proximity. I say comparative for the Moslems were prudent enough to specify many remote events before their Kiyamat and thus avoided the error of the earlier Christians in fixing it too soon. The *answer* in the text alludes to the examination of the candidate for heavenly bliss where a regular list kept every day and night by a pair of angels (invisible of course) on his shoulders, will be duly read out to him, and his destruction then be fixed. No wonder that the *"day* of Resurrection" is to last either 1000 or 50,000 years! But, in my humble opinion, both periods are either much too long, or much too short. Vid Sale's Prel. Disc. p. 64.

quietly, and seized two or three of the young birds. The vulture heard their cries and asked her why she had seized and brought them? The cat replied, "I too have two or three little ones, whom I have not seen for many days; of course my heart yearns towards them, and as often as I remember them I shed tears. For this reason I have brought these young things, that seeing them in the place of my own offspring, my heart may be occupied." The vulture believed her, and the cat devoured all the batch she had brought. Afterwards by thus bringing them one by one, and two by two, she ate them all, and when they were finished, went her ways. But when all the birds who inhabited that tree returned each to its own nest, all began to search for their young, and to ask who had removed them. After much seeking and enquiry they found part of their offsprings bones under the tree, and part in the hollow occupied by the vulture. Seeing this all made sure that he was the culprit, and rendered uneasy by the violence of *maternal affection*[79] they began to beat him, and vent on so long pecking at him with their beaks, that at last they killed the poor wretch.

After relating this tale, the crow thus continued "0 dear! such is the advantage to be derived from admitting a stranger into your abode." The jackal hearing these words became angry and said "0 crow! thy name is Su-budh, (good understanding) yet is thine intellect a very dull one, for thou art unable to comprehend that no one issues from his mother's womb with friendship for another. So when this deer first met thee, thou didst not know him, nor was he acquainted with thee; but when ye both began to inhabit one place, then your intimacy daily increased. The good believe all to be their friends, and only hypocrites and deceivers can instinctively distinguish between a well-wisher and a foe. We are all slaves of one household.[80] As the deer is my friend, so also art thou and perhaps even more than he is." "Of a verity, O Su-budh!" said the deer, "we are all brothers to each other; as in the *Glorious word*[81] even we find it

---

79 Literally, "rendered restless by the fire of their wombs."

80 "We are all God's creatures and servants."

81 The Glorious word is the Koran. The verse quoted "Innama'l mu-minun ikhwatun." "Verily the true believers are brothers." Koran. Cap. 49

expressed, that "all the Faithful are each others brothers." If this jackal desires to pass his days in conversation with us, *what do we lose by it?*"[82] Hearing these words the crow quoted the following Misraa.[83] "If my dear friends pleasure be in this, then all is well."

The night was passed in this conversation, the moon set and the sun rose. The three friends, namely, the crow, the jackal and the deer, went off to their respective haunts to feed. Every day, in this same manner they dispersed in all directions, and after feeding returned and passed the night in one place,—such was the tenor of their lives. One day the evil minded jackal, who was *watching his opportunity to devour*[84] the deer, seeing a fresh and green field of barley, in which some peasants had set a trap for antelope, ran up to his victim, and taking him aside said, "hear, 0 my friend! you are ever eating dry grass, and I cannot bear to see it; indeed it afflicts me extremely. Now today I just came from seeing a field of barley which exactly suits you, and in which you may browse at your ease, whilst my heart will be *gladened*[85] and my eyes *delighted*[2] by seeing you comfortable."

At break of day both started together, and when they had nearly reached the field, the jackal said to his companion, "now go and eat to your hearts content." The silly deer, seeing the verdure of the field, ran on without reflection and began to browse in perfect security. At that very moment he fell into the snare. The villainous jackal, in the joy of his heart, began to dance and violently to stamp with his *fore*[86] and hind feet on the ground. The deer thought

---

82 i.e., we lose nothing by it.

83 The Misraa or hemistich, is half a *bait* or distich.

84 Lit. "had placed his teeth on the deer's flesh, and remained constantly in that position."

85 Lit. "my heart will be cool"—i.e. I shall be joyful, for affliction is compared to a fire in the heart. So also when they say my eyes will be light," they mean that they will no longer be dimmed with tears. Both phrases are common idioms in Hindustani, as well as many other Oriental dialects. See page 54 note 122.

86 The forelegs of most quadrupeds are called *"hath"* or hand in Hindustani, as in Persian they use the word *"dast"*, in Arabic *"yad"*, and in Greek. So an elephant's

that these were signs of sorrow for the accident which had happened to him, and knew not that the *Sufi*[87] was dancing at the prospect of the table cloth being spread. "Friend," said the dupe, "why thus allow your grief for me to overwhelm you? Know you not that by the grace of God your teeth are sharper than a sabre's edge? Why do you not cut through the strings of this snare?" "O apple of mine eye," replied the other, *"hand and heart are at your service,*[88] but to-day I am fasting and this net is of leather; by biting it I fear lest my fast become *impure.*[89] It is now midnight, but to-morrow morning I shall not fail to act as becomes my intrinsic worth. Thus passed that night. In the morning, Su-budh the crow saw not his old friend the deer. He became thoughtful and said to himself *"last night*[90] my friend returned not home; all this appears not to me to betoken good. Had I not better see what the matter is?" Thus saying he began to search in every direction.

---

trunk is called in Sanscrit his (hasta) कार (kar) or hand.

87 The words (sophos) Sufi and (philosophos) failsuf, have fared very badly in the East; the former being generally used to denote a greedy fellow, a wolf in sheep's clothing; and the latter a cunning knave, a Sceptic etc. see D'Herbalot under *"Sofi."*

88 Lit. "I am present with my head and eyes;"—i.e. my head (or life), is ready to be laid down for you, and your order is upon my eyes,—the most tender and precious part of the body.

89 The Moslems divide all actions into five kinds -
    1st halal, lawful opp to 2d haram, unlawful.
    3rd Mustahabb, what is pleasing in God's sight, though not absolutely enjoined— it is opposed to.
    4th Makruh, an action displeasing to God though not absolutely a sin if done.
    5th Mubah—an indifferent action.
    Here the word Makruh is not used in its proper religious signification; for chewing anything as betel leaves etc, smoking and snuffing, render a fast batil, or nill and void.

90 Literally "to-day at night"; which phrase is not a *"bull"* in Hindustani whatever it may be in English. For with the Moslems the day includes the night, and the latter precedes the former.

At last to his horror he espied the deer, caught in a snare. Striking his head against the ground, and breathing out a loud sigh he began to say, "did I not tell you that this evil minded jackal is a villainous brute? This is the day of misfortune which awaits him, who hearkens not to the advice of his friend. "Where now is thy friend the jackal?" The deer replied, he is probably lurking about somewhere greedily awaiting my flesh." "Well," said the crow, "what was to happen has happened. Now pretend to be dead, and stop your breath, until I give the word; then arise and fly." The deer did as the crow advised him. In the mean time the owner of the field approached, and saw a fine fat buck lying dead in the snare. He lamented much, exclaiming, "how good it would have been had I caught this animal alive!" and very slowly cutting the tie which confined its neck, placed it on one side, whilst he himself set about raising the net. Thus the deer found itself at liberty, and when the crow gave the word, it rose up and fled.

When the peasant saw the buck running away he flung after it a club which he held in his hand. This accidently struck the head of the jackal, who was lurking about the spot thirsting for his dupe's blood. The wretch died upon the spot, but the deer escaped in safety. The wise of old have said, who ever diggeth a well for his brother, falls into it himself.

Whoso for others diggeth a fall
Himself shall fall in it first of all.[91]

In a word the deer and the crow met once more, and were both filled with joy. The latter said to the former, "know that the conduct of a foe is very like the gnat's ways. He first alights at your feet, then climbs up your back, and finally settles upon and hums in your ear. If he finds your body unprotected or espies a hole in your clothes, there he thrusts himself, and begins to suck your blood. So also acts the foe, what he cannot effect by violence, he will try to do by gentleness; he will humble himself at your feet, softly whisper in your ear, and

---

91 "He shall fall himself into his own pit" says the wise king. The Arabs still repeat their prophets saying "Man hafara bi-iran li akhihi, vakaa fihi."

endeavour to establish himself in your heart. As soon as he finds a weak place anywhere, he will work his will and pass on."

In a word when the mouse had finished his tale he exclaimed, "0 crow! I well know that you thirst for my blood." The other rejoined, "by eating you my life will not become eternal, nor by this means should I obtain imperishable wealth. Know the following assertion to be true,—that I desire your friendship with heart and soul, and wish to be on the same terms with you as Chitra-Griv was; for never did I behold so faithful a friend as you are. It is always better to enter into intimacy with the good, for they resemble the sea in their qualities; *deep*[92] as the latter is, so are they, and as no one can warm the ocean by casting fire into its waters, so too the good are not to be annoyed by any evil or misfortune. I well understand your character, and value your worth, being in fact enamoured of your good qualities." The mouse answered, "I have already several times told you that friendship cannot exist between us. Any such connection would be like the union of fire and water. However much the former carries the latter in a pot upon its head and warms it, yet does not the water cease its antipathy, and no sooner do the two meet, then the fire is extinguished by its foe. What reliance can be placed upon you, O crow? Your heart is as black as your coat,—moreover I am your food, and wherever you meet with a mouse you devour it. What bond of amity can I contract with you?"

"I have heard your words," said the crow, "yet am I not the less determined to engage in friendship with you, and should you not accept my offer, I will fast at your door, until the parrot of my existence flies from this cage of *earth*.[93] You are of an excellent nature, and I am confident that should we become friends,

---

92 This is a kind of double entendre, as the Sans. adj. Gambhir, means "deep", as water, but is also used metaphorically for grave, sedate, serious.

93 This practice was anciently very common in India and was called Dharna, or Dharna baithna. For a full description of the Dharna See Asiat. Pers. vol 4 art 22. The crow here threatens to starve himself to death, unless the mouse consents to receive him as a friend; and then the latter would commit the sin of murder. The vital principle is compared to a parrot, and the body to a cage of earth. As regards the word *"parrot"* it

difference or distinction could never arise between us. The friendship of the vile is as an earthern pot, with the slightest blow it may be crushed; but the intimacy of the noble-minded resembles a *copper vessel*,[94] which no degree of violence can break, and if perchance any where damaged, can be readily repaired. Most animals and quadrupeds become our friends, because we feed them. The foolish and the ignorant choose their friendships for greedy and covetous motives. But the wise and the intelligent meet together through kindness of heart. Such is your worth, that though I have wandered all over the country, yet I never beheld so faithful a friend as you are. For which reason I am anxious that the tie of friendship and the bond of amity, may subsist between us."

The mouse's heart was quite melted by these words, and he left his hole. Having met the crow he exclaimed, "O dear one! thou hast as it were poured sweet water upon the withered tree of my existence, and greatly gladdened my heart. You are now the friend of my soul; approach and allow me to clasp you to my bosom." Both animals embraced and showed many signs of joy. The mouse entertained his friend with much attention, and when they had finished eating and drinking, the former crept into his burrow and the latter retired to his own place. And ever after, the two friends were in the habit of meeting every day, and after wandering in all directions in search of food, they used to pass the night together. Whenever the crow found any delicate morsel, he generally would bring it home to his friend. Thus these two spent their days on that plain.

After a short space of time, the crow began to say "my friend! nothing to eat

---

may be observed that most of the modern languages of Europe derive the word from the Spanish and Portuguese, *Papagayo*, which is taken from the Arab. *Babagha*.

94 In some other versions, it is much more appropriately compared to a golden vessel. But the Asiatics though generally speaking devotedly fond of metaphor, have not restricted themselves by anything like European rules in their use of that figure. What they are particularly addicted to, is *straining* it as much as possible, and never for a moment think of puportioning the dignity of the simile to that of the object compared. Thus a man is likened to a louse, to a gnat, to a chess-man etc etc., and the less probable, or rather the more harsh, forced and unnatural the metaphor appears to European, the more it seems to suit the Asiatic taste.

or drink can now be found hereabouts,—and if found, it is with much toil and trouble. It is at present my wish to leave this for some other place, and removing there to pass our lives happily." The mouse Hirannik thus answered him; "Hear, O my friend! without seeing or hearing anything about it, why seek another habitation? Wisdom requires that we first search for an abode, and if we meet with one that suits us, then desert our old home,—if we cannot find a more suitable place, it is better to get through our day as well as we can here." The crow replied, I have seen a spot, and fixed upon it for our residence." The mouse asked him where it was. He answered, "there is a jungle called *Dandak Karan*,[95] through which the River *Cavery*[96] flows from the north southwards. Mathurak[97] the tortoise, an old friend of mine, has been dwelling there for the last twelve years. When we arrive there, whatever food we may usually require, that we may ask of him whenever we want it, and through his intervention, the Almighty, will certainly supply us with our daily bread." "If" said the mouse, "you have made up your mind to cease dwelling in this place, it offers no inducement to me to continue in it alone. Take me also with you. For the wise of old have declared that, wherever a clear-sighted master, learned discussion, a man of intellect and foresight, a just governor, a clever physician, and an intimate friend cannot be found, that place we should not select for a residence or a home. For on a former occasion, my crony Chitra-Griv, the King of the pigeons departed, and I remained behind alone. After this event you became my intimate, and now you too wish to leave me. How then am I to get

---

95 (दाण्डका) Dandaka.s.f. or (दाण्डकारण्य) dandakaranya s.n. the Peninsula of India, from between the Nermada & Godaveri Rivers to the South, the whole of which in the days of Rama, was a large forest. The name is derived from danda s.sm. n.a. stick, and (अरण्य) aranya. s.n. f. a forest. This forest is most celebrated in Hindoo mythology as the habitation of Viradha, the mighty demon, and the scene of great events. Vid Ramayana B.I. Sect 7.8.

96 A River in the Deccan, called in Sans. (कावेरी) Kaveri s.f.

97 In the Hitopadesa, the tortoise is called Manthara S. adj. Slow, tardy,—a sufficiently appropriate name for the animal as is proved in Page 64.

through the long days of *solitude*?[98] Friend, if you depart, take me with you too." When the crow heard this declaration of the mouse's, and both had agreed in opinion, they set out together for the Cavery River. The tortoise saw the two advancing from afar; being much delighted he went on to *meet them*[99] and affectionately enquired after their health and welfare. When the crow had returned the salutation, the tortoise asked him, "who is this companion of yours?" "This," answered he, "is that mouse, to whose virtues a thousand tongues could not enable me to do justice, and his name is Hirannik." Then the tortoise a second time embraced them both with the greatest cordiality.

(The crow remarked) there is a proverb that the old, the young, and even children,—in fact every visitor or guest,—must be treated with civility and politeness; for their claims to attention are admitted by every breathing thing.

There is also a saying, that if an inferior enter the house of a superior, the latter is bound to behave courteously to him. He (the crow) then related the whole tale of Chitra-Griv, after which the Tortoise entertained them most hospitably, and after serving meat and drink to them, he addressed the following

---

98 This dislike of solitude is Moslem not Hindoo. The latter from peculiarity of religion, customs, etc. appears in his domestic habits, a rather unsociable animal. The former is quite the contrary, and hates solitude during the day for its discomfort, and during the night for its dangers. There is a popular superstition that jinns often visit those who sleep alone, causing madness and other accidents. The Arabian Prophet was determined that his followers should consider living in the world as part of their faith, and struck at the root of monastic institutions by declaring, "la ruhbaniyata fi'l Islam" "there is no monkey in Islam."

99 This going out to meet a visitor, is called istikbal in Arab. Pers. and Hind. In all three countries, the distance to which the master of the house moves, in receiving one whose rank claims the honour, is precisely fixed by the rules of ceremony. There are no greater sticklers for these minutise than Asiatics in general, and our European ignorance of, and contempt for such matters, are infinitely distasteful to them. In a position where a foreigner is thrown into close intercourse with natives of the East, it is absolutely necessary to study the customs of their society a little, unless he desires every day to offend by apparent neglect and incivility, and to make himself ridiculous by misplaced attention and politeness.

question to the mouse. "Peace to your *honour*,[100] why did you abandon your home and come to dwell in this vast jungle? Pray explain the circumstance at length." "Hear me, O lord of the River! said the mouse, there is a mountain by name Chandra, at the foot of which is a populous village, called *Champapur*[101] the majority of the inhabitants of which are *Jogis*.[102] I had dug my hole and used to live in the house of one of them, named *Churakaran*[103] whose practice it was every day to go and beg in the town, and to bring home with him grain cooked and uncooked. After eating and drinking, whatever might remain, he used to place upon a lofty *shelf* in his room, whilst I thrusting my head out of my burrow, used to watch his motives. But when he slept I would creep out of my hole, and springing upon the *shelf*,[104] would go and stay there. I then used to eat as much as I could in perfect security, and destroy all that remained. I

---

100 This word *hazrat* is Arabic and Persian, especially in the latter language is generally applied to their Prophet and his successors, and very sparingly used as a term of mere politeness.

101 In Sansc. (चम्पकवती) Champaka-wati. The word s.f. Champa is the P.N. of the Capital of the Prince Karma, the situation of which is said to have been somewhere near the modern Bhagalpur. For the meaning of the affix Pur, see page 9 Note 8.

102 The Sansc. has (परिव्राजक) Parivrajaka. s.m. an ascetic, religious medicant. The Jogi in Sanscrit Yogi, is supposed to be a doctor, who abandons the world for the purpose of spiritual worship of God, and the practice of a certain form of devotion which unites the soul with Brahma, or the supreme Being. Such is the theoretical signification of the word. The practical is a dirty rascal who practices upon the credulity of the superstitious vulgar, and would rather beg than work.

103 Chura s.s.f. (चूड़ा) is the single lock of hair left on the crown of the head at the ceremony of tonsure. Karan s.s.n. signifies an act or action. Chura-Karama s.s.n. is a rite performed in the 2nd or 3rd year after the childs birth, and purifies him, by removing all the hair except one lock on the crown. It is the eighth of the 10 Hindoo Sanscaras (संस्कार) or sacraments for the three first classes of Society, commencing with the garbhadhanam, or sacrifice on conception, and ending with vivaha or marriage. In the Hitopadesa, the word is written Chura-Karna.

104 This word "tak" is Arabic, and though occasionally signifying a shelf, is more often

never used to stir out of the house, but there used to pass my life.

One day, Chura Karan the Jogi taking up a club, approached my burrow, and began to rap at its entrance. At that very time *Bina-Karan*[105] an old friend of his, entered the house, but the master of it was so much taken up with the rapping, that he never once turned towards him. The visitor said, "I have come here to meet you, and in the hope of enjoying your society, whereas you sit there with a club in your hand to frighten me." Then Chura-Karan's wife, seeing the state of the case, said to her good man, "to-day after a long time Bina-Karan has returned; treat him with politeness, enquire how he is, and tell him how you are getting on yourself." Chura-Karan replied; "this action of mine is not ill-timed for in this same burrow is a mouse, who, whenever I place my eatable upon the shelf, springs up there, eats all it can and wastes the rest." Bina-Karan replied, "just show me that place;" the other said, "look, here it is." When Bina-Karan had seen the shelf, he said, "this place is too high for even a cat to be able to make such a leap. This can never be without some good reason. Perhaps in the place under this, where he dwells, there may be a hoard, for such powers can only be accounted for by the possession of wealth.[106] So likewise when the Banyan's young wife gave her husband several kisses in rapid succession, this action of hers was not without a cunning intention." Chura-Karan asked what that story might be, and Bina-Karan commenced . . .

used for a recess in the wall, where dishes, provisions and other such articles are generally placed.

105 In the Sanscr. (वीणाकर्ण) Vina-Karna. The Vina, or Welna, is a kind of lute or guitar, with 7 strings or wires, of about two octaves extent, the invention of Nareda the son of Brahma. It is very celebrated in Hindoo poetry, and being almost as good as a bad guitar, is attributed to a celestial inventor, as the lyre was by the ancients to Mercury.

106 This is completely an Oriental theory; that the possession of wealth influences the possessor and urges him to undertake great things. It is however sufficiently correct.

The Tale of the old Banyan and his young Wife.

In a certain province of Hindustan, is a town in which dwelt one *Chundrasain*,[107] a very wealthy Banyan, who was about a hundred years old; and there, too lived a young woman called *Kelavati*[108] , the daughter of a Banyan. So beautiful was she, that the Sun and Moon became uneasy when *they gazed upon her,*[109] and the humble- *bee*[110] was put to shame by the glossy blackness

---

107 For an explanation of this word vide Page 9 note 9. In the Hitopadesa, the Banyan's name is Chandan-das, a much more appropriate one; for the affix Sain belongs to the Kahatriya caste. The Banyan or Banik, is the 3rd or agricultural and mercantile tribe, and wears the so called Brahminical thread. Yet the affix das (by us usually written doss), properly belongs to the Sudra or fourth and servile caste, though now almost always assumed by Banyans. In translating the word Banyan, they generally employ the Arabic Bakkal. A shopkeeper, grain merchant. As regards the *moral* of this tale, the less said about it the better; its object seems to be to prove how much is generally done, for interest's sake.

108 Why the lady's name is so much altered, I cannot say; in the original it is (लीलावती) lilawati s.f. a sportful woman; from (लीला) s.f. a branch of feminine action proceeding from love, and consisting in the imitation of a lovers manner, gait etc., to pass the time during his absence. The passion of Sringara, or love, was a favourite subject for subtle definition amongst the ancient Hindoos, the moderns treat it much more cavalierly. For a short account of it, see the Prolegomens to Wilson's Hindoo Theatre. Vol 1.

109 A fair specimen of Persian bombast, translated into Hindustani. The meaning is, that the lady so much surpassed the Sun and the Moon in brilliancy and beauty, that those two lights were rendered restless and uneasy by jealousy when they saw her. This use of the figure Hyperbole is inordinately common in Persian, and eloquent Hindustani.

110 In Hind. bhanwar. In Sanscr. (भमर) Bhramara s.m. from the root (भ्रम) bhram, to roam or wander. It is a large solitary bee, exceedingly black and shining rather of a blue, or indigo tint than otherwise. In Hindoo poetry etc, it is supposed to be enamoured

of her looks. With her *narcissus*[111] like eyes, she enchanted the whole creation, with the *bewitching arch*[112] of her eye-brows, she made mankind distracted and with the glitter of her teeth she conferred lustre upon royal *gems*.[113] Now the grain seller in the insolence of riches, had actually married this beauty; but as he was extremely old, and she was just grown up to puberty, she was not very happy in the society of her antiquated lord. One day she saw a handsome young Banyan whose name was *Manohar*,[114] and falling in love with him at first sight, thus addressed him "hear Manohar!; I am sinking in the sea of *youth*[115] can you not

---

of the Kamala or lotus and is used as a general comparison for the hair. It is almost needless to remark that in India and central Asia, only the blackest locks are admired; brown hair is generally given to the Rakshasas or demons, and the lighter tints are known to be peculiar to the Mlenchchhas or barbarians, who cannot speak Sanscrit, and are not subject to Indian institutions.

111   The Narcissus in Persian is supposed most closely to resemble the human eye. So as a proof of king Mushirawan's modesty he is said never to have caressed his wife before that flower. The word Shahla is the feminine of the adj. Ash'hal from the trilit verb. Shahila, (the eye) was black with a tinge of red. It is used as an epithet to Nargis.

112   Literally "the sorcerer-deceiving bow," thus comparing the lady's eye-brow to a bow, and the effects of it to magic, which outdid all other enchantment. Yadu is here used in its old sense of a sorcerer, as we often find it in the older Persian works.

113   This most extravagant idea is continually met with in the Persian authors; and the meaning (if it has any) is that such is the lustre of the truth in question, that all gems derive their water and brilliancy from them.

114   A Sanscr. adj (मनोहर) sig pleasing, lovely from Manas, the mind, and hren, to take, or steal.

115   Youth or rather puberty, is here compared to a sea, and love to a ship or vessel. The meaning of the lady's metaphor is very clear, but as the author does not choose to confine himself to the metaphorical, I shall be obliged to leave out a portion of the original and slightly alter other parts. Of the Hindustani word Joban it is as well to remark that the Sanscr. (युवन) Yuwan is an adj. sig. young—hence the Pers Jawan—the Latin Juvenis, and the other modifications of the latter word in the mod. lan-

seize my hand, and draw me into the vessel of your love?" With fervency he replied, "yes indeed, I too desire to become your lover, by some means or other, for since many a day my heart has been entangled in the *noose*[116] of affection."

The two lovers began to take the greatest pleasure in each others company, and thus passed the time very happily. One day Chandra-Sain returned home at an unusual hour; and unfortunately it so happened that Manohar was in the house at the time. Kelavati saw that her secret was likely to be discovered. She instantly arose from the couch, rushed to the threshold of the door and seizing the hair of her goodman's head, kissed his face four or five times in rapid succession, and taking his hand led him into a corner. Manohar seizing the opportunity, and avoiding the husband's eyes, escaped from the house. But when the lady saw that he was gone, she gave her husband a *kick or two*,[117] and cried out, "O nasty old man! will you ever treat me with this unkindness?" She then in a passion threw herself upon the bed, and drawing the *sheet*[118] over herself from head to foot, went to sleep. "And thus," pursued *Bina Karan*[119]" as the young lady's kissing the old man's face was not without a reason, so also this mouse's spring is not without some cause."

---

guages of Europe which are derived from the Latin.

116 This kamand was a rope with a noose to it, anciently used in war for scaling walls, unhorsing a foe etc., Most of Firdausi's heroes fight with it, and though now it is of course quite disused with the Ancient Persians it appears to have been a favourite weapon. Manohar compares his heart to a warrior who has been entangled in the coils of the Komand.

117 Lit. "Two or four kicks." The lady's speech is utterly unfit for translation, but it contains an excellent reason both for the kisses and the kicks.

118 The word *"Chadar"* which for want of a better I have translated *"sheet"*, means the long thick veil with which women cover themselves in the streets, as a kind of over-all, and also use as we do a sheet when sleeping, with the exception that the head is never left exposed.

119 In the Bo. edition of 1835 we find Chura-Karan here for Bina Karan,—a mistake; for the latter tells the story, and it is for him, not for the listener, to deduce its moral.

In a word, the two *Jogis*[120] drew some chalk from their pockets, and after drawing upon the ground certain lines after the manner of astrologers, they found out that at all events there was property in my burrow. "For if not" (said they), "how could a mouse have such power? The possession of wealth only give great strength,"

Gifts become the wealthy man,
Distress pursues the poor man.
Gold it is that makes a man,
The gold-less man is no man.[121]

Then the Jogis with a mattock dug down into the hole, and took from it the whole heap of my Rupees. Now this property had been collected by my ancestors and myself, still they seized every stiver of it. I soon perceived that when they had thus appropriated my wealth, no strength and power remained in me. I immediately became as one stupified, but the days of my life were not fated to end here; by this means precious existence deserted not this earthly frame. O King! in the first place my hoard went, secondly the Jogis began to revile me. Grieving for my wealth, and stung by their insults, *my heart was consumed*[122] and became as ashes. For this reason, I left house and home and came to seat myself at your *feet.*[123] "Tell me friend," said the tortoise, "what bad language did they use to you?" The mouse replied, "they said that had this property belonged to a respectable owner, he never would have been so thrifty

---

120 In addition to the remarks made in Page 35 note 71. the student may consult the account given of the Jogis in the Dabistan,—a work now translated; but he must always recollect that the author was a Mussulman, and that his statements, however amusing, are many of them quite incorrect.

121 This sentiment is certainly the very populi in other places besides India; but we should define the distinction thus. Poverty is said to be a misfortune in most parts of Europe, but a sin in England;—in India it is a crime of the deepest dye.

122 "Consumed" (by the fire of affliction),—for any tribulation is compared to a fire in the heart. So also the active verb Jalana lit. to burn, to light signifies to afflict, torment.

123 Vide Page 35 note 71.

and chary of it;—he would have made a far better reckoning in his economy. This mouse must be a most ignorant and foolish animal, thus to have manifested his powers. For instance, the wise of olden time have said, whoever shall obtain wealth, either without trouble, or by the strength of his arm,[124] and who shall not himself spend it, nor allow others to spend it,—neither give it away himself, nor cause others to give it, then shall he have utterly thrown away the pains he took in collecting it, shall suffer punishment for it gratuitously, and be called a miser and wretch throughout the world. That man's name no one would pronounce as he rises in the *morning*;[125] but rather make it a perpetual subject of reviling,[126] and abuse all his fellow countrymen for his sake. With such and similar conversation, reproaches and revilings, they used daily to afflict unhappy me, till at last I was utterly unable to endure their bad language." "Friend", said the tortoise," afflict not your heart. As they remarked to you that the miser's life and death are the same, so too the wise have declared,

> *Only for spending's sake, my son, the glittering ore esteem*
> *The hoarded gold & hoarded stone, of equal value deem.*

It was well, O brother! that that property was lost to you, otherwise some one might have murdered you for your money. *In a word*[127] you have, thanks be to

---

124 "The sweat of his brow," as we should say.

125 See Page 16 note 30. Asiatics are all very early risers, and the dawn of day besides being considered the most pleasant part of the twenty-four hours, is held by Moslems to be the most Mubarak, or propitious. There is an idea in Persia, that the blessing which attends the sheep's offspring, and prevents their being entirely destroyed, is in consequence of that animal's early rising;—whereas the dog who dozes at dawn of day, in spite of its numerous young, and its never being slain for food, never multiplies beyond a certain point. The idea would have been new to Buffon!

126 Literally "people will never smith with their slippers upon his name," a metaphor expressing insult or contumely; as there is nothing more degrading than to be beaten with slippers or shoes.

127 The Pers. adv. bare is very badly translated by, "in a word", or "at last." It has exactly the signification of the French "Enfin." As regards the prediction of the

God, escaped in safety; you will still possess property in plenty. Whoever trea-sures up wealth but spends not proportionably, must expect the very same accident which happened to you." The mouse replied, "what? do you also, like the Jogis, insult me with your sarcasms? However without worldly goods a man is nothing whatever. For instance, let a rich individual enter another's abode as a guest, without any previous acquaintance, still people will show him civility without end, whereas if the *poor*[128] and indigent go to the house of even their friends, no one will regard them. Wealth is an excellent thing."

A penniless man is always the slave of a *woman*.[129] Until a man restrains his hand from profuse expense, and secures his purse strings with a firm knot, wealth will never remain with him. O my dear friend! when by the oppression of the wretched Jogis I found that all my goods and property had gone, my abode became empty indeed, but still I continued to exist there in any way I could. Yet reflecting that in this world there is no such friend as money; that it is equal to our parents, and perhaps superior, since, by some means or other, it never fails to supply our wants; that, in a word, nothing in the world can get on without it; I said in my heart, it is no longer advisable for me to remain here,

---

mouse's future wealth in the next line, this is a polite form of wishing him good fortune. It is used both in conversation and in writing.

128   This word "gharib" in Arab. & Pers. as applied to men generally sig. a stranger, one out of his own country. In Hindustani it is also used in the two senses of poor, (e.g. gharib admi, a poor man); and tame, quiet, (as gharib ghora, a quiet horse).

129   Meaning "inferior in dignity and lower in the scale of creation than a woman." This for an Oriental is a considerable fall, for the phrase, "less than a woman denotes something very low down in the ranks of humanity. The words "kam az zan basham" "may I be less than a woman" are beautifully introduced into the eloquent lines attributed to Sultan Togh-rul, and beginning with,

Ai dil! be-hava e Arman ar man basham,
Khali na kunam az to, Kam az zan bisham,
O heart! in my desire for Armenia, (if I only live so long),
Should I not expel thee, (i.e. his foe) *may I be less than a woman*
See Nigaristan Bo. ed. P. 165.

and this is not a story which should ever be communicated to strangers. Even so it is said that a man, if wise, will conceal three things as much as possible. In the first place, any loss of property; secondly the wickedness of his wife; thirdly, any grief which his heart may feel. I have thus explained my misfortunes to you, because you are my friends. (To proceed), when I lost all power of leaping, I was compelled reluctantly to leave my old home, and to take up my abode in a jungle on the banks of the Ganges. In a word, many thanks to the Almighty, that I have been permitted to reach the shade of your *protecting skirt*.[130] Truly it has been said that the world is like a *poisonous tree*,[131] and that the Almighty grants the attainment of five things to those upon whom he would have mercy;— namely, daily progress in learning,—steadfastness in worship,—knowledge of the heart,—veracity of speech,—and the friendship of the good. My heart, 0 tortoise! is not grieved by the injury done to me by those wretched Jogis, since my life is safe and I have met with such a protector as you are. For the loss of my property is very little evil, since in this world all things are attainable. Worldly riches are not to be depended upon; at one time they come, at another they go. "Brother," said the tortoise "whoever gives the *regular alms*[132] out of his wealth, that man's treasure fails him not, nor has any one the power of meddling with it. Even as the wise of old have declared, who ever dams up flowing water, and leaves it no way to escape in even the smallest quantity, little by little it will collect, break through the dyke however strong, and thus

---

130 In the original, "daman i daulat," the skirt of your happiness i.e. *your skirt*. The skirt is alluded to because a suppliant generally seizes that part of the garment; hence such an application is called daman-gir-i, or skirt-seizing. The word *"daulat"* is prefixed, in polite phrase, to the names of objects belonging to a person addressed, e.g. daulat - khaneh, *your* house—etc., etc.

131 Our old idea of the Upas is not unknown to the Orientals, but they do not confine themselves to one tree. The tamarind, for instance, is considered certain to cause fever in those who sleep under it, and many others are more or less calumniated.

132 For a full account of the Zakat, or Alms, consult Herklot's Qanoon -e - Islam. Chap XII. The word is derived from the irregular Trilit. Ar. verb, *Zaka* he was pious or pure; as such donations are supposed to purify the remainder of one's property.

all flow off. So too it is with wealth, whoever toils to collect it, but spends it not, and gives it not away in charity to anyone, his fate is that his property shall eventually be spent by others,"

> *Part of thy riches spend thyself, and part to others give,*
> *And store up part for other's sake, if happy thou wouldst live!*

O my friend! the rich miser is the keeper of wealth, not its master nay, a thousand times happier is the *beggar*,[133] who, whatever he gets, much or little spends it without a thought, and at night reposes peacefully in the bosom of his family, nor admits into his heart any kind of affliction. He who is at once rich and a miser, must pass every night in fear for his hoard and his life, lest any one take away the latter in his desire for the former. But have you never heard of the tale of the Jackal?" "No," replied the mouse, "relate it to me, friend, I am anxious to know what it may be." The tortoise began in the following words . . .

---

[133] Regarding these fakirs or Dervishes, see Herklot's Qanoon - e Islam Chap. 28.

History of Artha-lobhi[134] the Jackal.

There is a city called *Kalyan-pur*,[135] and in that place was a Governor, named *Parman*.[136] One day it so happened that he mounted his horse, and rode off to some jungle in search of sport. The first thing he espied as he was

---

134 Artha-lobh is a compound Sansc. n. masc. signifying Avarice. In the Hitopadesa, the jackal's name is Dirgha-rava s.m.f.n. howling, yelling fr. dirgha adj. Long, and (राव) rava, a cry.

    The object of the following tale is, to impress upon the mind, that favourite piece of Oriental advice, "that the greatest folly in this world is to collect money and not to spend it." The theme is more hackneyed in the East than in the West; for where there are no funds or saving-banks, in fact, no means of preserving property the thief, the solutua hoeres or the Ruler generally manage to divide it between them. The Arabian Prophet said bashshir il bakhil bihadisin mu warisin "Convey to the miser the glad tidings of accidents and heirs!"

135 (कल्याण) Kalyan S.s.n. happiness, prosperity, gold—fr r. (कल्य) Kalya, healthy and (अ) to be.

136 The Hitopodesa says, "there was a Vyadha, by name "Bhair-ava." The Vyadha is a man who lives by hunting deer and also a low, bad fellow. Bhairava is the common name of the eight inferior manifestations of the Deity Siva. It is to be remarked that although in the heroic ages and amongst the Kshatriya races, hunting was a favourite pastime, yet in later times the Hindoos generally speak of it as a mean and servile occupation, always making the huntsman of low caste, and giving him some horrible name. On the contrary, the Moslems look upon the chase as a royal pastime, and indeed in general are most inordinately fond of it. The preserves of Seind would have excited the envy of William the Conqueror, and the hunting parties of the Tartons are conducted upon a scale of preparation which astonishes Europeans. See Petit de la Croix's life of Genjiscan 1.3.c.7. and for an account of an Indian battue see the Tale of the Four Dervaysh Appendix—Malcolm sketches of Pers. vol. 1. Chap 5. Burckhardt's notes on the Bedouins and Wahalys Vol. 1 pp. 220 et sex. and Burnes's visit to the Ameers of Scind give full particulars of the sport in these countries.

riding along, was a fine fat deer, on seeing which he quickly dismounted, and discharged an arrow at it. The shaft no sooner struck the animal, than it fell quivering to the ground, and the sportsman raised it upon his shoulder, and went in the direction of his horse. Just at that moment, he saw a large hog coming straight towards him. In his avidity he removed the deer from his shoulder, and placing it upon the ground, edged a little way out of the road, so as to avoid being seen by the animal. At last finding an opportunity, he shot it also with an arrow. The hog no sooner felt itself wounded, than in a paroxysm of fury, it managed to kill its destroyer with its tusks, and then fell dead itself. In a word, Parman the sportsman, the deer and the hog, all three lay lifeless on the same spot.

An hour or two afterwards, Artha-lobhi, a certain jackal, arrived at that plain—Great was his joy; after many thanks to the Almighty "never" cried he "before to day have I been able to obtain such exquisite dainties as these. I will now, for some days to come, eat as much as I can in peace, and dry some of the parts to be kept for *Kababs*.[137] Well, the *covetous*[138] brute fixed upon this project, and first began to gnaw the bowstrings. But the bow being tightly strung, no sooner was the cord cut through, than one of the horns struck the greedy jackal's breast with such violence that *he died upon the spot*[139] and thus since the covetous animal could not eat that prey, but preferred hoarding it and beginning with the bowstring, what fate had prepared for him happened to him. Whoever shall collect wealth, it is his duty to spend a part of it, and to keep a part of it, and to give away a part in charity. You however did not act thus; you threw away the whole in vain. Now however do not lament the loss. "Brother," said the mouse, "the case is as you say." "Friend, continued the tortoise, if you pine

---

137   The dish which is usually called *"Kabab"* in the East is made of small pieces of roast meat, with onion between the bits, served up upon a skewer. But the Persians use the word *"Kabab"* for any roast meat, as the French say "un roti."

138   The author has used this word haris more than once, for there is a well known tradition of Mohammed's "Al hariso mahrum." "The covetous man is disappointed."

139   Lit. "He never even asked for water"—a favourite phrase as the first thing that a wounded man cries for is for water, in these climates.

for your hoard, you will suffer the wretchedness of grief, and probably die in consequence of your vexation. Then men will jest at you, and say, "how sensible he was, thus to throw away existence for the sake of wealth!" Rest assured, if life be preserved, property to any extent may be acquired. O mouse, proceeded the tortoise, "had the jackal eaten up all that flesh, his case would never have been such. In a word since you *enjoyed not your property, grieve not for it now*.[140] For it is said, when the nails of the hands and feet, the teeth and the hair of the head leave their places, they become mere nothings. If you grieve for the loss of your cold, your flesh will fall away, and your bones become like *lime*.[141] In the service of the Lord continue so steadfast, that the world may become as it were your slave. Do you not see, when a woman conceives, before the child is born God Almighty creates food for it in the mother's breasts? Now that omniscient Being is the Giver of daily bread to both of us. O friend! Consider this shade as your own, and live with me." When Lakh-Patank, the crow, heard all this humility, he began to praise the tortoise[142] and said "if an elephants stick in the mud of a river, none but an elephant can extract him from it. Thus too, when this noble mouse is involved in such misfortune, he comes to you, for you too are of high family." After this conversation, a hearty friendship was struck up between the mouse, the crow, and the tortoise, and all three began to inhabit the same place. One day they were much astonished to see a deer by name *Chitra Lagh*[143] rushing in flight towards them, and as soon as they beheld him, the three friends fled also. The tortoise took to the river, the mouse crept into his burrow, and the crow flew up into a tree. But when the latter had looked all around, but saw no one in pursuit of the deer, as soon as he reached

---

140 The Hindustani here, has the advantage of the English, "Since you eat not your property, do not at least eat grief."

141 This word Chuna is der. from the S.s.m.n. which sig. powder of any kind, as well as chalk or lime—hence our barbarous word *chunam*. The meaning of the passage is that "The violence of the fire of affliction will melt away your flesh, and burn your bones."

142 Literally, "loosed his tongue in praise of the tortoise."

143 The name is utterly corrupted probably from Chitra s.n. painting and the r (लक्ष) laksha; spot mark. In the Hitopadesa it is (चित्राग) Chitranga S. adj. Spotted, marked.

the place the crow called out, and hearing his call the three friends met together. First, the tortoise said to the deer, "no one was in pursuit of you, what made you run in such a hurry,—is all well with you?" He answered, "it is in fear of the huntsmen that I fled hither in such a state of agitation, and now it is my intention to pass the rest of my life in your society." The tortoise looked towards the mouse, and the latter said, "since you come here in fear, so now be of good cheer, and allow no thought of evil to enter your mind. You are now our comrade. O friends! the deer and our three selves are now sharers of good and evil." Hearing this, the fugitive was highly delighted, and seated himself under the tree close to his friends. The tortoise asked "who are these huntsmen, and where did you see them?" He replied, "I heard that the Raja's sons, who govern the country of *Katsk*,[144] have alighted with their suite upon the banks of the Bhagirathi River, and will visit this lake to-morrow for the purpose of fishing in it. "Hearing this, the tortoise's heart palpitated with fear of the sportsmen, and he began to remark, "if to-day I remain in this lake, to-morrow I shall be consumed by the fire of hunger, that is to say, they are pretty sure to carry off all the fish, and I must die of hunger. It is better than for me to remove to some other *lake*."[145] The crow and the deer agreed in opinion with him, but Hirannik, the mouse, after some reflection said, "it is difficult for the tortoise to travel by land,— if it could only manage to go by water, it would arrive quite safe. For thus it is said, aquatic animals are powerful in their own elements as men are defended by the walls of a fort. My friends! if this tortoise be allowed to go by land, you will all repent your action, even as the Banyan regretted his own handiwork." The friends enquired what the shopkeeper's story might be, and the mouse thus proceeded with . . .

---

144   (कटक) Katak. in Sansc. s.m.n. an army, camp, city or town.
145   talab, is the Persian, and thil, the H. word for what we generally call a tank, i.e. a basin of water, larger than a pond, and smaller than a lake. The word "tank" is, I believe, Portuguese, "*tanque*" a cistern, but it is now used both in writing and conversation, in the Hind. Mahr. & Guzerati languages. The word talab is der. from the S.s.m. (talla) a tank, and ab water from the Sansc ap.

The Tale of an Individual called Tankbir[146]
and Naujobana[147] the Banyan's Daughter.

In the city of *Cannoge*[148] there was a Raja called Bir-sain,[149] who founded a city which he named after himself, Bir-pur, and made a certain Tankbir, one of his servants, Governor of that place. About a month afterwards, the latter set out to visit his town, when he saw Naujobana, the daughter of Banyan, standing at the *window of her house.*[150] No sooner did he see her than he felt himself stung by her *snake like*[151] ringlets, fell from his horse to the ground, and instantly fainted away. His people put him into a palanquin, and conveyed him to his own house. His fostermother[4] asked him what the matter was. He

146 This individual's name has no meaning in Hind; in Sansc. from turang s.s.m. a horse, and (नुरगबल) form, figure, strength—In the Hitopadesa he is a Pajaputra or prince.

147 Meaning, "Just grown up to puberty," (a girl)—See Page 52 Note 115. The Hitopadesa gives (लावन्यवती) lavanyavati, which may be changed from (लावण्य) lavanya s.s.n. salt-ness, beauty, from (लावण) lavan. salt.

148 In Sansc (कान्यकुब्ज) Kanyakubja, or (कान्यकुब्ज) Kanyakubja (signifying the crooked or humpbacked maiden.) the ancient Canogyzan. The name alludes to a very improper action of the Hindoo Deity, vayu or Pavana, for an account of which, see Moor's Hindu Pantheon Art, Pavana p. 321.

149 In Sansc. (वीरसेन) Virasen, the name of the father of Nala-Raja. The word (वीरा) vira is a s.s.m. a hero—heroism, valour. May not the Latin vir, virtus etc be derived from this r. or from (वर) vara, the Sansc. adj. excellent?

150 The Sanscrit version has (सवहम्यं) Swa-harmya. Swa from Sans, one's own—harmya S.s.n. s palace, the abode of a rich man. The *window* is of my own insertion.

151 Literally, "the female snake, or Cobra capella of her locks." Here the lady's zulf, (as Pers term, sig. a ringlet) are compared to a snake, on account of their form, glossi-ness and power of fascination. So Hafiz likens the ringlets of his beloved, to an af'i (asp, or viper). As regards Tank-birs extreme sensitiveness, it may be remarked, that

replied, "my eyes fell upon a beautiful maid, whether fairy or mortal, I know not. *The thorn of her rose-tree pierces my eye*,[152] and from the pain of that wound I am now suffering." The fostermother thus learned that her boy had been hurt by the shaft of Naujobana's charms, and began to scheme how she might best bring about an interview between them. At length, she found some pretext for repairing to the lady's house. On arriving there she was astonished to find her also wounded by the danger of her lover's beauty, and suffering from such agitation, that she retained not strength even to move. The nurse whispered very softly in her ear, "O Naujobana my Tankbir is weeping on your account, and lying upon his bed as one distracted. If you would only assist in curing him with a single kiss, I will give you a golden *taka*."[153] "Silly nurse," replied the other, "go to another shop for that article!" The old woman then began to

_____

such cases, though they appear tolerably ridiculous to a European, are frequently quoted in the East. For there are no people who admire exaggerated and almost unnatural descriptions of the tender passion, more than Orientals, and that, perhaps is no bad proof of how rarely it really exists amongst them. None of our old novels which treat of chivalrous love, can equal, in their grotesqueness, the Eastern tales of Layli and Najnun, Khusraw and Shirin, with many others—See Lockett's Commentary on the Mint Amil P.P 63. 67. 172. Also Lane's Arabian Nights in almost every chapter. As regards this tale there is one in the Arabian Nights (Vol 2. P 61. 62) of a bathkeeper, his wife and a young man, which, in the *point* of it, very much resembles the story of Tankbir, but the Moslem's language and ideas are infinitely more gross than the Hindu's.

152 As we should say, "my eyes were dazzled by her beauty." Beauty is very naturally compared to an arrow, sword, dagger, or any such weapon; being the armour and defence of a woman.

153 The *taka* is a copper coin, worth 2 paisa. Here it must mean two ashrafi, or Mohurs. This offering money is perfectly characteristic of the East, where a man can do nothing with an empty hand. A native of India once informed me that he was a perfect Perhad, (a Romeo, and most devoted lover) but that he feared that his fate would compel him to abandon the world and become a fakir—I asked him if nothing less would make the lady relent. Oh, said he, sufficiently naive, she wants an Ashrafi, but are mera bap re! where can I get the money.

apologize and said, "my flower of a boy is fading away in the sunbeams of your love, and by the shadow of your charms only can be restored to its former freshness and beauty." "Nurse," said Naujobana, "*my husband is the guardian of my garden.*"[154] Hearing this, the nurse was silent and returned home. When Tank- bir saw her, he said you have put the spoon in, *where is the sweet-meat?*"[155] in other words, where are the wages of toil in the service of love?" She replied, that she had prepared everything in the most knowing way, but that patience was necessary for a few days, as the lady was in fear of her husband. "Still," added she, "I have a remedy for all that, and will so manage, that the good man shall himself bring her to you. Hear! of my child! things are effected by contrivance and intellect, by violence they are never brought about. That, have you never heard of the story of the jackals, who, by the force of intellect, managed to devour a live elephant?" Tankbir asked what that might be, and the nurse proceeded with . . .

---

154 The metaphor will readily be understood. This sentence however, admits of two meanings, either that the lady was determined to be faithful to her husband, or, as is here meant, that his watchfulness prevented her infidelity.

155 A Persian sentence, meaning, "you have toiled and laboured, what are the results?"

The Tale of Dhul-tilak[156] the Elephant, and Atma[157] the Jackal.

It is related that in a certain jungle called Dandakaran[158] was an elephant in rut named Dhul-tilak. The jackals were anxious to find out some means of devouring his flesh after two or three months, and one of the multitude, called 'Atma', thus addressed them. "Friends! I will bind this elephant with the chains of wisdom, and smite him with the shafts of contrivance." After these words he went forth in haste, and when he approached the elephant he salaamed to him and respectfully *stood at some distance*.[159] The other asked him who he was, and whence he came. He replied, "the Kings of all the animals and

---

156   Dhul S.s.f. dust. and Tulak S.s.m. the sectarial mark, generally made upon the forehead, with coloured earths, sandal wood, etc. The epithet may sig. "one having the Tilaka of dust." In the Hitopadesa, the elephant's name is (कार्पूरतिलक) Karpura-tilaka, i.e. one having the Tilaka of Camphor. (from Karpur s.s.m.n. Arabic Kafur, Greek Kaphoura, Latin Camphora. not from the Hebr. Kapara "because it signifies heunah"). The fam. of this word, "Karpura-tilaka," is the name of one of Durga's female attendants.

157   Ataman m. (atama f.) the self, the abstract individual, the soul, the intellect. Hina the Gr. Autme and the Pron. autos, which enters so much into compound words.

158   The story of the Elephant and the jackal, illustrates the superiority of intellect over bodily force, numbers or size—a favourite lesson in the East. Saadi says in the Gulistan Chap 1 Tale 3 that "one Arab horse, however lean is more valuable than a stable full of asses." By the Hindoos the elephant is much revered, (though there is some uncertainty about what caste should bury him,) but the Mussulmans consider him unclean, as we read in the same chapt. of the Gulista "the sheep is pure but the elephant is carrion." The common word for an elephant in Hindustani is hathi in Sanscr. (हस्ती) hasti, meaning, "the animal with a hand," from (हस्त) Sanscr hasta,— the hand.

159   To show the difference of rank; for in Oriental society the farther one stands or sits from the master of the house, etc etc, the lower one's rank is.

of the jackals, have sent me to wait upon you with this message, that they desire to elect you Raja of this jungle. If you accept the offer you will be pleased not to delay for a moment, but come as quickly as possible. Both monarchs with all their attendants, are expecting you." The elephant in his delight followed him with all speed. The deceitful jackal led him by a lake, in which was a quicksand, and not being heavy himself, he passed over it by treading very lightly. Then standing on the other side of the lake, he called out to the other to come *straight across*,[160] as there was very little water. The elephant was so weighty, that he sank into the quagmire the very first step. He then asked his friend what he was to do. The jackal said, "hold on by my tail, and I will *extract you from the stream*.[161] Fool! replied the other, "your strength can never save me. "Then," said 'Atma', "if you allow me, I will summon hither my tribe, who will draw you out of this quagmire." The elephant, after he had stuck in the mud, soon became tired of struggling and stamping with his feet, and was as one who,—floating in the water, sees bits of straw swimming about him, and stretches forth his hand, *in the vain hope that thus he may be saved*.[162] But what can an insignificant straw do for him? So Dhul-talak, in his stupidity, exclaimed, "very well! go and summon your friends, that they may extract me from this calamity." The jackal ran off, and presently returning with the whole of his brethren; himself stood right in front of the elephant, whilst the rest of the party attacked him in the rear, biting and tearing his flesh. The unhappy animal exclaimed, -

"Thou didst sowed in my heart the seed of love,"
"But what was in thy heart at last appeared;"
"O heart of stone! to win my heart for this purpose"
"That such a design was in thy heart, my heart ne'er feared."

---

160   Literally, "straight opposite your nose."

161   This speech of the jackal's does not proceed from stupidity or derision—it is prompted by that truly Oriental wish to conceal his cunning and villainy, under the disguise of symplicity and want of understanding.

162   The Arabs say,—"the drowning man catches at every straw."

"Thus 0 Tankbir! continued the nurse, "you have seen that by the force of his intellect, a jackal destroyed an elephant. And do you think that by my natural talents, I cannot even manage to make your love affair end happily?" "0 fostermother!" said he, "the *falcon*[163] of my heart is in pursuit of the bird of Naujobana's charms, for which reason the hue of health has fled from my cheek, and rest from my heart." At last the nurse whispered in Tankbir's ear some such words, by the obeying of which success would be ensured to the seeker, and then went to her own house. He (as she had advised,) sent for Naujobana's husband, took him into his service, promoted him to honour, and intrusted to him delicate and important affairs.

One day, Tankbir thus addressed him, "friend! last night I saw a vision a woman mounted upon a *lion*[164] who told me that if every day for one month, I send for a woman to my own house, dress her in brocade and gold cloth, place my sash round her neck, and *fall at her feet*,[165] then dismiss her, my life will be a long one, and my prosperity will increase day by day. Moreover whatever woman comes to me and departs in the gold cloth, she shall certainly have a

---

163   The lady's beauty is compared to a bird, and the lover's heart to a hawk in pursuit of it. The shahin, is, I believe, the male bird, and bahri the female of the same breed. In Hind. and Pers. the male and female of the same kinds of falcons have very different names; e.g. baz the female falcon (gen: called shah-baz, or royal hawk)

      Jurrah, the male. lagar s.f. the female of jhagar s.m. the male of a kind of kestrel. The other hawks usually found are the chargh, (much valued) the basha, a female bird (not the male as it is given in Shak. Hind. Dict) used for partridges m.The chatua and its female the turmati. See Burnes's visit to the Ameers of Scind and Malcoms sketches of Persia vol 1 chap 5.

164   For the word Sher see page I have translated it, "riding upon a lion," because as all the personages in this tale are Hindoos, the allusion may be to the Goddess Durga, who has many names denoting her being represented riding that animal; e.g. (सीहयावा, सीहरया) Sinha-ratha (fia (सीह) lion).

165   Not to be taken exactly in a literal sense. It generally denotes to, "entreat submissively"; also to join the palms of the hands and raise them to the forehead. For a description of the patka, which I have rendered "sash", see Qanoon.e Islam Append. p. XII.

son and her husband live to a good old age. And further more, (she told me) that if I could not manage this, Naujobaha's husband, my servant, is doomed to death, and that I also should not escape. Now say, what must be done?" The Banyan replied, "let it be your business to bring me the woman, and I will take charge of clothing them in the brocade." When night came on, the Banyan brought a female to the house. Tankbir took her off to his private apartment, whilst the shopkeeper, concealing himself, began to look out with the intention of seeing how his master conducted himself. There he saw him dress up the woman in a suit[166] of brocade place his sash upon her neck, fall at her feet and then dismiss her. Seeing these circumstances, the Banyan said in his heart, "this Tankbir is a great fool for thus giving her gratis all this brocade." But when he and the woman left the house, he *demanded*[167] half the cloth from her. She replied, "why, Tankbir gave it all to me, what right have you to it?" In a word they quarrelled so violently about this, that the woman's clothes were torn to rags, and she in return pulled out half the Banyan's *beard*.[2] When Tankbir heard of the affair, he laughed heartily and knew that in a day or two his suit would be successful.

The Banyan related at length to his wife all the adventures of the night. She said, "you must have taken some low uneducated person there, for had she been a respectable woman such a disgraceful affair would never have occurred." The shopkeeper that night, took a female of some consequence to the

---

166 What we call a "suit" the people of India term a "pair" (jora) of clothes, because they generally wear two articles the men a coat and pajamens (or drawers), the women a cholis (bodice) and Sari. The Hind tash is a corrupted form of the Pers tas, or Tash. The Badla or Badleh is a H. Word.

167 As his dasturie, or perquisite. But the demand is rather exorbitant.
Notes 2, 3, and 1 on next page
The Mussalman author of this story, not wishing to introduce a brother Moslem taking his wife to another man, has made the hero of the tale and his dupe Hindus; But as usual it is full of incongruities. Banyans wear no beards, and have no day of resurrection (kiyamat), moreover they make but little distinction between *mahram* and *na-mahram*, (which I have translated "*strangers*").

house, and Tankbir behaved to her exactly as he did to the former one. Seeing this, the Banyan began to feel some regret. On the third day he said to his wife, "O Naujobana! all this money is being thrown away to no purpose. If then you will only *accompany me*³ there, one single night, all this wealth will come into your hands." The lady answered, "there is no reason why I should go to the house of a stranger." But the Banyan who reposed great confidence in his spouse, said to her, "as soon as you arrive, Tankbir gives you a suit of brocade, falls at your feet, and then dismisses you." Naujobana replied "the woman who obeys not her husband habitually, will suffer the punishment of her offence on the *day of judgement*.¹⁶⁸ I only desire to please you, and what ever you say, the assent to it be upon my head and eyes." The Banyan was delighted when he heard these words, and said to his wife, "the blessing of God be upon your father and mother!" When the wandering sun had travelled over the plain of heaven, and arrived at his corner in the West¹⁶⁹ about the end of the *first watch of the night*¹⁷⁰ the foolish Banyan, in his desire of gain led his wife to Tankbir, as he had before been accustomed to take other women there. But when the latter saw her, he was highly delighted, took her into an inner room and said "O Naujobana! the army of *cruel love*¹⁷¹ had utterly laid waste the land of my heart; now at length, by this visit, it will once more be *happy*."¹⁷² The Banyan, who

---

168   Explanation given on page before.

169   i.e. "When Evening came on". This comparison is much more natural and pleasing than that in Page 41.   and it sounds familiar to us, as in almost every language the Sun has either been represented as, or compared to a traveller.

170   The pahar (fr the Sansc. (प्रहर) prahara. s.s.m.) contains eight gharis, or about three hours. There are therefore four pahars to the day, and four to the night. The first watch of the latter would be from six to nine P.M. The words pahar-rat exactly express the meaning of the Latin Vigilice.

171   The original has "Kafir" literally, an infidel, a Caffre; metaphorically a mistress. Here it is used in a kind of amorous abuse, and may be translated by *"cruel"*

172   Literally "populous inhabited," but in the text it refers to the kingdom or land, to which the lover compares his heart.

was, as usual standing there in concealment, hearing these words became ashamed of his action, and beating his head returned home. And thus, my friends! if the tortoise go by land, even as the shopkeeper repented of what he had done, so will you. But the tortoise's heart was much troubled by the news respecting the sportsmen, which the deer had given him, not acting therefore upon the counsel of the mouse, according to the advice of the deer and the crow, together with them he left the lake and set out upon the journey. It was necessary for all three friends to accompany him, so they followed close behind him. With a thousand difficulties they had got over about a Cos, and were desirous to rest under the shade of some tree, when they were horrified to see a Shikari advancing towards them with his bow and arrows. The friends instantly dispersed, each in one direction, the crow went and sat upon a tree, the mouse crept into some hole or other, and the deer fled into the jungle. But the tortoise being an aquatic animal, and consequently unable to make his escape by land, remained upon the same spot. Then the Shikari seized him, fastened all his four feet, hung him to the horn of his bow, and went on towards his own house. But when the three friends saw that the tortoise was taken, they began to weep and the mouse said "brethren! did I not tell you that if this tortoise go by land, much trouble will be the result? Your sighs and lamentations are now of no use make some contrivance, by means of which our friend may escape." The crow and the deer said "0 Hirannik! without your intellect and management, *his release is clear*."[173] "0 deer!" said the mouse "go ahead of us, and wherever you see a pool of water, pretend to be lame and stand still. When the archer approaches you, fly from him limping and very slowly." The deer did exactly so, and as soon as the man carrying the tortoise appeared at the water's side he saw a lame deer going along. The tortoise being heavy, he placed it upon the ground, and pursued the other animal. When he had advanced about a bow shot, the mouse coming from behind, cut the noose which bound the tortoise, and called out to the deer, that the captive was now safely lodged in

---

173 Meaning that "his death is certain" but not wishing to use so ill-omened a phrase. See Page 21 note 44.

the water, and to make his own escape. The deer acted accordingly but when the Archer returned from his vain pursuit to his great disgust, he found not the tortoise anywhere. Repenting of what he had done he said, "the wise of old truly declared that whoever abandons the half in pursuit of the whole, attains not the whole, and loses the half. Thus if I had not followed the deer, the tortoise would not have slipped out of my hands." The Shikari went on grieving for his loss, and all the four friends, after a joyful meeting, declared that the place in which they met was a suitable one, and that they had better remain in it. So the Mouse, the Crow, the Deer and the Tortoise, all built their abodes, and dwelt in that same place.[174]

When the Brahman had concluded his account of Mitra Labha, or the Acquisition of a Friend, the young Princes were highly delighted and exclaimed, "Such then, Maharaj[175] are the advantages to be derived from amity and affection! Greatly have we been benefitted and admonished by hearing this story."

---

174 Not contented with this, the Guzerati Panchopakhyan States, that the four animals above mentioned, at last obtained their (गती) or salvation.

175 See Page 13 note 21.